The Cannibal

by

Jesse Bier

Cover design by Debby Florence

Edited by Mackenzie Cole & BJ Soloy

milltownepress@gmail.com

This is a work of fiction. Names, characters,
and incidents are the product of the author's
imagination. Any resemblance to actual events
or persons, living or dead, is entirely coincidental.

milltownepress.com

The Cannibal

CHAPTER ONE

"They put Sypher up against the BMW–arms leaning over the top of the car, legs spread apart–and searched him. One of the officers felt something, all right, in both pockets. And backed off. Thought they were bullets. Well, what would anybody think? They said, 'Empty your pockets. One at a time: leave the pockets hanging.' Sypher did it on the right side, then on the left, and put his hands back on the roof. Instead of bullets there were three human fingers lying on the road by his right leg, and two by the left. The officers felt–"

"Never mind!" Robert said. "Spare me that whole scene. The question is, why are you getting into it again? I want to know. As your friend. Not an analyst. It seems a little bit–"

They had been playing chess again, at Sculli's house.

Cole said, "–sick?"

"Indisposed, anyway. Morbid certainly. Forget the unsavory details, and just tell me your motive. Why are you interested in it again? It happened a few years ago."

"It was the one story that, for the little I had to do about it, I was sloppy on. Listen, I've just been made Special Investigative Reporter and Assistant Editor for the paper–a transition until I take over as Editor. I want to pick an old story I'm a little ashamed of and re-do it so that–"

"–you can move on, confidently. You have to justify as well as satisfy yourself?"

"Maybe."

Mrs. Sculli came in with coffee and homemade crumb cake. She waved a hand and left them to their game, which was finished, and their talk.

"Robert," Wilbur Cole said, "there's something I want from you in this."

Sculli poured the coffee, cut the crumb cake and served.

"I am not going to psychoanalyze dead men," he said.

"All I want to do, from time to time, is bring up this or that side of it and talk to you about it."

"Why can't you find colleagues on the paper?"

"They won't do. All the more now. But you'll do. Not as my personal psychiatrist, or substitute father, or even an adequate chess partner. Only as my friend."

"Leave me out of it."

"Just a preliminary question."

2

"No," Sculli said. "Anyway, I never agree to anything and start in on it at the same time."

"I just want to know, for something to think about, what cannibalism means."

"For openers–just a full-scaled theory?"

Cole had to smile. But he persisted. "It's not just the act of ultimate destruction?"

"No. It's also an act of incorporation, after all."

"A sort of ultimate compliment as well as annihilation?"

"Yes. Actually it's a sort of supreme neurosis–if you define neurosis as the incapacity to decide, or the wanting to have something both ways. Neurotics are like children. But children are passing through a stage. Neurotics, then, are like permanent adult children."

"And cannibals are the primitive children of our race?"

Probably Sculli agreed, but he did not reply.

Cole asked, "But why would a *modern* man…?"

"I quit! I don't even recall his name–"

"Sypher, Virgil Sypher: 24 years of age, from Butte, right here in the state: mostly a drifter, but with no record of violence in his past."

"All I know is that he wanted to utterly destroy and yet be a part of. In a moment of hysteria, probably."

"What does that mean?"

"Exactly? How would I know? You have to get the facts again."

"Yes. I'll be accumulating all sorts of notes." Cole got up. "I can incorporate these ideas."

"There's that word again," Sculli said, standing and shaking Cole's hand for good night.

CHAPTER TWO

In the *Missoula Tribune* office Cole now had two desks. He had one immediately to the right as you came in the double doors and went around the switchboard girl, Sally, to an office behind her fronting the street: Fleming's office, fitted with another desk for Cole. And as you went on by Sally and turned left and proceeded down a long aisle, passing the Editorial desks on the right and Women's and Features on the left, there in the back the aisle narrowed and you found the reporters' desks massed to the left, with the Composing section still farther back, and on the right three desks for the City news, the State man and the Western region editor and a fourth for Cole as Investigative Reporter.

Heinz and Stoddard and Forbis were on site in their vaudeville mode. Heinz said, "Here comes the fair-haired boy."

Cole elaborately paid no mind and sat down.

"No," Stoddard said, "too bald."

"Just scanty," Forbis said, "not really bald. That's not fair."

"Who said fair?" Heinz kept it going. "I said fair-haired. All right, he's the scanty-haired boy around here."

"Not a boy. Old, old. Did you catch that worried, prematurely old look in his tired eyes?"

"Maybe he was just up late. Hell, let's leave the poor old balding son-of-a-bitch alone."

On his desk calendar Cole took note of a memo about a 9:30 interview of a working apprentice or protégé for him from the Journalism School. He had time to go to the Files Room and put a spool of microfilm on the machine and turn through that one summer and start reviewing the Sypher crime. He got up. Ray Unruh came bustling in from somewhere and sat swiftly at a desk across the aisle.

It was a different desk every week or so for Unruh, since he was hired just for the summer to fill in for vacationing regulars. Now in early September the vacationing was just about over, and he was desperate to find a permanent job somewhere, anywhere. He had lost his job as an English instructor at the university in Missoula and, in a tight college situation now, could not find another place. Luckily he had some experience on a newspaper in Wisconsin and had taught for one year in high school and supervised the student paper, so when he came down to the *Tribune* on an outside chance for work in June, Fleming had him see Cole, and Cole had hired him to fill in. By now, Cole had become his mentor and was sending reference letters around the Northwest for him and could maybe squeeze out another month or so for him at the *Tribune*, but that was all.

"How's it going?" Cole asked.

"BOR-ing," Unruh said. "Would you believe it, I'm in Obits today."

He was mercurial, too. Up to now he had been enthusiastic no matter what the assignment, happy not only to have a job but showing genuine delight over the machinery, especially the new Video Recording Terminals everybody at the paper had now. For an ex-English instructor, in particular, hitting the "h-j" key for "hyphenate and justify" and watching while the message went to the control computer and came back to the VRT unit, resizing the story and re-hyphenating according to its memory bank of *Webster's Abridged International Dictionary* and placing it all on the little green and yellow screen right before your eyes, made Unruh smile every time and sometimes laugh outright. Until lately.

6

Now he said "BOR-ing" about most things, but he meant "DESPERATE!" And there was little you could do for him.

"Well," Cole said about the Obits, "at least you're not in them. Always remember that."

He went to the Files Room.

CHAPTER THREE

For July 12, Cole read–

MAN'S TORSO FOUND IN BLACKFOOT RIVER

BONNER – The torso of an unidentified man was found in the Blackfoot River Saturday afternoon about four miles north of Bonner.

Cole sat back up for a moment. He blinked in the dark of the Files Room, hunched over the microfilm viewer. He thought, why, after a clear headline, do we repeat ourselves in the first paragraph? He leaned back into the visor and read again.

The torso–minus head, arms and legs below the knees–was discovered by Felix Rhinehart while fishing at Johnson Creek, where it empties into the Blackfoot.

...recovered by deputy sheriffs...in the water not more than 24 hours...clothed only in a pair of shorts.

The river bank and adjacent area... searched for additional evidence...an investigation was begun by the office of Missoula County Attorney Richard Coheen, Sheriff Len Boucher, and Coroner Myron Corette.

The very next notice, Cole saw, carried the AP bracket and he recalled that Herb Wilson was assigned to the story for national wire coverage. Cole skimmed–

LITTLE PROGRESS IN TORSO CASE

BONNER (AP) – Autopsy...disclosed...victim was a man in his early forties and weighed approximately 200 pounds...

Missoula County officials organized a search...no clues have been found so far...

Corette said a hatchet or saw had been used to dismember the body. "It would have required two people or a person of considerable strength to carry out such mutilation," he said.

The break came a day later, on victim and criminal both.

MAN HELD IN BIZARRE CASE
Livingston Man Torso Victim
By Herbert Wilson

MISSOULA (AP) – Bruce Dahl, 40, formerly of Livingston, has been identified as the victim of murder and cannibalism in a crime destined to become a memorable...

Meanwhile, a wild-eyed young man arrested outside of Sacramento, California, has confessed to the crime. Authorities reported he had human fingers in his pockets.

He is Virgil Sypher, 24, of Butte, Montana. State Highway Captain Jack Miles says Sypher has signed a statement in which he admits eating the heart of his victim, after killing him on a secluded road in western Montana... He claims he had some sort of electrical accident at 16 and hasn't been the same since...

9

Searchers from Missoula County Sheriff's office believe they have found what they think is the scene of the crime. They have found a blood stained 14-inch knife...

Later, Miles says, Sypher, a hippie type, freely volunteered to talk about the crime.

"I have to listen," Miles told this reporter. "But I can hardly stand it. I've been 21 years in police work, but this?"

Cole got up and switched on the room light. It was all too pat. And Wilson's predictable style intervened. Still–Cole found Sally and asked her to turn off the machine for him and rewind and file the microfilm. It was 9:30 and, out again in the broad sun-filled newsroom, he was happy he had somebody to see.

CHAPTER FOUR

He was even happier than he expected, because the apprentice from the Journalism School was trim and pretty Mavis Ridpath. She sat at his news desk and they talked about what she would do. She had fine eyes, a slightly pointed chin and a good smile. She was serious, good-looking and alert. Cole liked her.

"You'll be doing simultaneous things," he told her. "I want you to get interviews with someone at the university on coal gasification figures. And you'll research something called toxic salt that they're putting in lamb patties for coyotes–"

She made a face.

"–no, it's all right–this is just to sicken the coyotes instead of kill them, to discourage them from raiding sheep. Here." He handed her a slip of paper with two or three published sources on it.

She smiled. She was really a lovely girl.

"Oh, one other thing," Cole said. "I'm also re-investigating a previous crime, mostly for myself. But from time to time I'll want you to do this or that on it."

"What's it about?"

"A man by the name of Sypher killed a man by the name of Dahl, up on the Blackfoot, a few miles out of Bonner. Then he apparently ate him."

Mavis Ridpath, who had been sitting very prettily and straight in her chair, almost slid off.

"No, no–I'm over-dramatizing," Cole said. "Maybe he just ate his heart."

Mavis still slumped somewhat in her chair. Her lips were parted. She was not smiling.

"If it seems as if I'm trying to jolt you some," Cole said, "that's only because it's true." He grinned at her. "It *is* an unusual case, but on the other hand, only a degree more than you're going to live with from now on... I tell you what–I'll put you on the easier parts. OK?"

"OK."

They both stood up. He shook her hand.

"Hey–" Heinz at the city desk prompted.

"Oh, let me introduce you around," Cole said. He did. Then she left.

Unruh came over to him. "I couldn't help overhearing..."

"Come on, Ray. You meant you couldn't resist overhearing."

"Have it my way," Unruh said. "All I want to know is, why am I on Obits or the Sunday Supplement or the Religious Page, when I could have one of the assignments you gave her?"

"Because," Cole explained, "they're my own assignments, and she's just my assistant. She's not being paid, Ray. These are her last credits at the Jay School, that's all."

"Oh."

"Which of those stories would you have liked?"

"The coyotes or the murder."

Cole nodded. "I thought so... Anyway, stop eavesdropping." He turned to the other three as well. "Everybody, stop eavesdropping. Don't you have any real work to do?"

"Uh-oh," Stoddard said. "That's the front-office Assistant Editor talking." He sat down heavily and plunged into copy and master-sheets. "*I'm* all right, it's the rest of you big-eared, lazy bums he's talking to."

Unruh was going back to his current desk, too.

"By the way," Cole asked him, "didn't you think she was pretty?"

Ray Unruh turned around. "Oh, yeah," he said. "Sure."

He probably meant it, too. Only, Cole understood, first things first.

CHAPTER FIVE

Cole spoke to Robert Sculli on the phone that night.

"I'm embarrassed by the sloppy reporting then, even mine. For instance, after Wilson was down with the DTs: there was a North Side call to the police–about a dog with a big strange bone. By the time a patrol car arrived, there was no dog around–only the human leg bone. Left leg. Identified later as Bruce Dahl's. There was no record kept of the person who called. And there was no knocking on a few doors by cops– or me–on the chance of locating the caller, to identify the possible dog owner, to discover where the dog usually roams, and so on. Anyway, what was part of the victim's body doing 25 miles from the murder site? You see, sloppy work. Maybe I was too close to it in some way then. What? The 14-inch knife? No, it wasn't the murder weapon; Dahl was shot."

"Ask about castration some time," Sculli said.

Cole didn't say anything. He looked around the room he was in. Then he said, "And there's the way it ended. I mean not that Sypher drove so far away, but so fast, finally, making almost sure he'd be pulled over."

"I don't know–especially at this time of night."

"Sorry. I'll call you earlier next time. Pleasant dreams."

He had to hold the phone receiver away from his ear, while Sculli denounced him.

CHAPTER SIX

At the *Tribune*, Ray Unruh popped an aspirin. Cole noticed.

"Don't you even want to take a drink with that?"

Ray shook his head. "Maybe I should open the bottom drawer, slip out the bottle and take a snort? Front Page stuff?"

"They say Herb Wilson actually had a little sign on his desk: Alcohol Kills Slowly: But Who's–"

"–In a Hurry?" Heinz finished. "Not bad. Did you see the Cambridge's new sign? 'Bar and Rest.' That's a period marking the end."

"If it only were," Ray said.

The others went on talking, about favorite signs.

"Gird up your loins," Cole advised Ray Unruh. "Mavis?" He called her over.

"Mavis has got to gird up her loins?" Ray looked her up and down.

Mavis looked back at him. Her smile came, sweet but delayed and indecisive.

Cole said, "Mavis, thanks for those reports on the Sypher story. I'm going to see the coroner and then the sheriff–the current one. I want you to see if the former sheriff–Len Boucher–is around anywhere and if he remembers something useful."

When she left, they all looked at her walking out. She was trim and brisk, but she had disturbingly full calves and there was the slightest swing to her hips.

"My headache's gone," Unruh said.

* * *

Coroner Myron Corette led Wilbur Cole into an inner office, where he went to a steel filing cabinet at the wall.

"Dahl–that was the name, wasn't it?" He found the folder and sat at his desk across from Cole. "I'll skim the report–and sound out some things for you." He had his selective delicacy, reading along to himself and then drawling out some facts. "Weight, about 200 pounds...but, uh, flabby. Amputation of arms, semi-crude. That means, not at the shoulder joints, but the slayer or slayers cut through the upper arm. There were...about twenty-seven knife wounds...most about two inches in length–"

"Hold it–can we back up?"

"You want *more* detail on the amputation?"

"No, no. But why did you say 'slayer or slayers?'"

"That's what I wrote here. Pre-trial notes."

"Only there wasn't any trial. Sypher pled guilty."

"Well, it's just proper procedure."

"I see. Do you still stand by the plural?"

16

"I was just being clinical, in supposition. It was *possible* for one."

"Oh. By the way, how did you people know it was Bruce Dahl?"

"He was somebody reported missing from work and home on the next work day, if I recall. There were five MPs reported in the state, only two men. Routine, Mr. Cole. We made positive identification by comparing X-rays taken of Dahl on a doctor's visit not too long before with some we took of the torso."

"Although there was a big chest wound?"

"Yes." He remembered or found it in the report he looked at again. "A gaping wound in the chest cavity...heart had been removed...only a very short stump of the neck remaining–"

"OK, OK."

"–and legs amputated at the knees. All right. *That* could have been done by one strong enough man. And Dahl was... forty-ish, flabby–"

"I'm leaving." Cole stood up, mocking his own squeamishness, but truly meaning to go.

"Imagine that fisherman who hooked the torso," Corette said. "He told the sheriff that he thought the body was a mannequin. He was sure it was a practical joke by some university students–a pretty sick one, but he was confident enough, fishing there with his four-year-old granddaughter, to reel in his pole and swirl the mass in to shore. When he saw it was human...Can you imagine?"

"Yes," Cole said, extending his hand. "That's my trouble."

They shook.

"I hope I've been of some help," Dr. Corette said.

"You have. I appreciate it. Thanks."

"Not at all. Any time."

Cole turned around at the door. "Oh, one more thing. Was Dahl castrated?"

Corette said, "Why–no." He made a move toward where the file folder still lay. "No," he remembered certainly, shaking his head.

It occurred to Wilbur Cole to ask Myron Corette another question entirely.

"Can I ask you something personal, Dr. Corette? Off the record."

"Go ahead."

"Do you like your work?"

"Yes. I like dissecting. Not cutting into live tissue. But dead bodies are, well, dead: finished, unfeeling. Cutting into corpses is not the same at all. I think most coroners would tell you that."

"And cannibals?" Cole's thought came out loud. "Sorry, I didn't mean that as a comparison. Well, bye."

"Good-bye. And good luck," Corette said.

Cole smiled suddenly. "You think I'll need it?" he asked.

* * *

He called up Sculli over the noon hour. Marge Sculli answered.

"It's Wilbur Cole. How are you, Marge?"

"Oh, so-so," she said. "Here's Robert. Say hello to June."

"Sure."

"Is that you, Wilbur?"

"Right. Just to say–have you had lunch? I can call back."

"What is it? Go ahead."

"Bruce Dahl. The torso case. Not castrated."

"Wilbur, Wilbur! Then it was substitute dismemberment, that's all."

Cole sighed, very audibly. "So you win, even when you lose? The old closed system."

"Now, now. Think about it. But not me: I need my nap."

"Just thought I'd tell you. Thought it would shake you up. I might have known. I'm heading for the sheriff this afternoon. I *won't* call you afterwards."

"Since it can make no difference? Don't be annoying. Just hang up quietly."

"Nighty-night," Cole said.

CHAPTER SEVEN

The present sheriff was Max Spahn, a big hulking man. He had a great puffy face and big ears, but steady eyes.

Although he hadn't been sheriff then, he recalled the case. And he retrieved the file.

"Dahl was shot–" Cole started.

"By a .32," Sheriff Spahn read.

"Where?"

The sheriff rifled through some pages. He looked up, faced Cole. "Doesn't say." His grin turned to a grimace. "Maybe in the heart. And the perp removed the evidence. Whew!"

"No other bullet wounds?"

"Not that we know. Listen, he said he shot him. He was in a daze–on LSD or something–and didn't quite know just where or how. What difference does it make? They had what was left of a victim, and they had their man. Who cares how exactly? Or even why?"

"I do, for one. Why not why? Let's go back to who. Were they absolutely sure Sypher was the one?"

"He had finger bones–the correct ones–in his pocket."

"Still, he could have been a witness. Strictly speaking."

"He was driving the victim's car."

"So they had him on auto theft."

"You'd've been the only one on any jury to find circumstantial evidence like that not enough to go on."

"Yes, they call it presumptive evidence."

"Sure. Hell, Mr. Cole, when you get right down to it, we never *know* anything for sure. The cops could get to a scene even when a shot was going off and not know if it was, say, justifiable homicide. You could know what and not who, or who and not what. Least of all, why."

"Ever find the gun?"

"Nope."

"Where did Sypher get it?"

Sheriff Spahn looked through some sheets but couldn't find anything satisfying. "He said he just had it there."

"Maybe it wasn't his. Maybe it was–Dahl's."

"I don't know."

"You didn't check?"

"*They* didn't check," Spahn corrected. Then laughed good-naturedly at Cole. "You mean it could have been self-defense, the killing part?"

"Well?"

"But the accused never claimed anything like that."

"It wouldn't have done any good if he proceeded to mutilate the body for some reason."

"So, he was guilty of something just as bad or worse."

"Maybe. I'm only trying to keep an open mind."

"As long as it ain't so open that nothing stays in, finally."

It was not an insult, just a matter-of-fact statement. Spahn spoke mildly. He was getting his big frame up. Cole wanted to hold him a little longer now.

"Just a couple more factual questions? Thanks. The knife–"

"A fourteen-incher–found stuck in a tree."

"Whose knife was it?"

"Sypher's," Sheriff Spahn said, adding in a weaker tone, "probably." He shrugged his shoulders. "What difference would it make?"

"I don't know. Maybe a lot, maybe none."

"Well, there's nothing more in here." Spahn looked up from the folder. "Tell you what. They keep all material evidence for ten years, over near the State Prosecutor's office, at a warehouse in Helena. I can get it back and we can look at it together. How's that?"

"Fine. Was there anything else found at the site?"

"I don't see–Oh, here: not very important—but some pieces of dark green plastic. No particular significance. Maybe not even associated with the crime."

"And that's all?"

"That's all."

"How come no alerts, no public notices, were ever put out on Sypher?"

"Why?"

"To find out–well, anything. Maybe somebody would have recognized that he was hitchhiking on that Blackfoot road the day before or that very day, since he evidently didn't have a car himself." Spahn was reading along meanwhile. "Was he, in fact, picked up, by anybody or *with* somebody, by somebody?"

Spahn found a notation. "You're probably out of luck–though you would have made a good policeman." He held up a sheet. "Virgil Sypher had been wearing a full beard–"

"So?"

"–up until the day of the crime, when he shaved for a job interview the Bonner lumber mill. Which he flubbed, by the way. After which, he went on upriver and subsequently killed Dahl."

"So references to hippie appearance were post-Manson prejudice. Or journalistic hallucination."

Sheriff Spahn seemed to read Cole's mind, or had been waiting with his gibe a long time. "The reporting was as bad as the police work?" he asked.

Cole got up slowly. "You know, there's a little bar just before that designated campsite by the river, a little upstream from where Johnson Creek comes in?"

"Yep." Sheriff Spahn stood all the way up this time, too. "There's a swinging-type footbridge across there."

"That's it. People fish around, residents go back and forth. Was the bartender at that bar ever interviewed?"

"In case Sypher ever dropped in, bearded or beardless?"

"Or Dahl."

"No—no record." Spahn reached down and closed the file. Again he asked, softly, "What for?"

"I don't know. Maybe Dahl had already picked up Sypher—alone or with somebody else."

For the first time Max Spahn's eyes widened and brightened. "You're getting me interested in a closed case, ancient history—and somebody else's at that. With my workload, this is ridiculous. And what for?"

"I don't know."

"You keep saying that. But you keep wanting to know what you probably can't know anymore."

"Maybe"

"And you keep saying maybe, too." Spahn spoke confidentially: "Granted, Len Boucher wasn't the brightest sheriff in the world. But I don't want to bad-mouth him. Would I have done different?"

"I think so."

"Maybe—now you got *me* doing it! —but I'll give you a call on that knife. You're on your own for anything else." They shook hands. "But you already *know* that," he said, grinning broadly.

Cole said thanks and good-bye.

CHAPTER EIGHT

Cole and Robert Sculli were driving up the Blackfoot canyon to go fishing, in Cole's car.

"According to Mavis Ridpath," Cole said, "Len Boucher knows or remembers less than Spahn. He got everything mixed up, including the fact–or the wish–that Sypher was the last man the state hanged. In his memory Sypher had stolen the victim's 'big Porch,' instead of small BMW, as the motive for the crime. What a great compliment to Montana civilization that, when they got their collective legal hands on Sypher at the airport, on extradition, they didn't actually string him up then and there."

"Finally wasn't Sypher put away for life?"

"Yes. But he didn't last long. That's another story–"

Cole pulled into the Blackfoot Tavern stop.

Sculli feigned perplexed surprise. "Eleven years of fishing together– and we've never stopped at this bar before."

"I seem to have a powerful thirst, all of a sudden."

"Sure. Powerful thirst for knowledge. But not all of a sudden. Premeditated. You hypocrite, you lug, you traitor. But why are you so compelled?"

"You think so? Maybe. But I'm caught up in it. Listen, there are philosophic as well as psychological sides to it."

"Oh, so you want a capital-A Answer now, as well as an explanation. They're not the same thing."

"Not to you. But for me, right now, at this stage of my life, yes. All right, I'm compelled. I want to know."

"Well, wanting so bad can become a case in itself."

"I'm taking the chance."

"So I see." Sculli sighed. "I'll stay in the car."

"Come on."

"The truth is you may need me to hypnotize the bartender?"

* * *

They were the only customers. The bartender was a burly man, who wore a pale orange western shirt with sleeves a trifle too long, and when he shot his cuffs it was as if he were aiming at whoever was right in front of him. Cole and Sculli took beers and, when the bartender slid over a dish of packaged peanuts and cashews, they each partook.

Cole said directly, "I'm reworking the cannibal case. Some years back." He took out his wallet for his *Tribune* card and laid it on the counter next to him. The bartender saw and nodded. "Did Virgil Sypher ever stop here on his way back or forth?"

The bartender shook his head. He came over and stood in front of them on the other side of the bar. He shot his cuffs. "MacIlhaney," he said and shook hands ceremoniously with Cole and Sculli. Then he leaned on the polished bar top.

"But the other one came in."

"Who?"

"The dead man."

"I take it," Sculli remarked, "before he died."

Cole said quickly, "Dahl. He was all alone?"

"Sure. He came in here askin' for information. He finally had a beer. Then I told him."

"What exactly?"

"That the fishin' was as good as they said. Your own paper, they was sayin' so. Matter of fact, it was good for business. There must've been a queer hatch on that year or something–the trout was bitin' like mad in the mornin's. I told him. He was headed for Great Falls. So he said. I happened to notice his foreign job through that window behind you, and they made a lot of that at the time. I told him there was a campin' spot just up the road a ways."

"Which he missed or misunderstood," Cole said. "Then he went a mile or so further, saw Sypher's campfire in that little turn-off up above and drove in there instead."

"And the chances are," Cole went on to Sculli, back in the car, "when you do climb back into your BMW and start her off, you settle into your little extra comfort for at least a mile's purring run, right? Everything contributes. So you don't turn off quickly–right about here."

Which is what Cole did, pulling his station wagon abruptly into the nearby public access and camping area.

"See?" Cole said. "I'm not taking you to the other place, where it happened. Just here, for fishing, as we planned."

"I'm spooked anyway," Sculli said.

They prepared to fish.

Cole said, "It'll be OK."

And it was. Although some retrograde cottonwood trees were putting some fuzz in the air and on the river, you could flick your fly into cleared pools and eddies. They both hit well. Cole caught a big one finally, and so did Robert, downstream from him. Cole walked that way. Then they both crossed a little cove, Cole steadying Sculli somewhat on the slippery rocks.

On the shore again he motioned to the landscape and sunshine. "Everything all right? You're not really spooked?"

Sculli shook his head agreeably.

"Relaxed?"

Sculli nodded.

"Good."

In the car, going back, Sculli said, "Also I repress well. One of my trout was a cutthroat, with a fair-sized minnow in his gullet."

"Ah?"

They drove on to Missoula. Not far from Sculli's home, Cole pointed out a mailbox sign: The Smith's.

"That gets me."

"The misspelling?"

28

"Sure. Also it's a curly-cued wrought-iron sign—our whole damn pretentious, misspelling, middle-class country hanging out self-advertisements of success."

"So you're in a sociological mood, too?"

"I just notice things. I'd like to put up a sign somewhere, called The Neanderthal's."

"For your information, the Neanderthals, however you spell them, were quite fine. Good people, probably kind. Even gentle. Maybe vegetarian."

"Is that a fact?" Cole asked. "What exactly are you trying to tell me?"

"Only that the wrong breeds won out," Sculli said. "Cro-Magnon— and cutthroat trout."

"You're your cheery self."

They drove a little farther without talking.

Then Sculli roused himself. "Aside from fishing, which I appreciated, what did we accomplish here?"

"We got into a discussion on self-advertisement," Cole answered, "including a nifty BMW."

CHAPTER NINE

Cole was reviewing one of his own back-number pieces at his newsroom desk with Mavis Ridpath. "Let's skim through it."

SYPHER CONFESSES

by Wilbur Cole
Missoula Tribune
and Associated News Service

MISSOULA (ANS)–Virgil Sypher...confessed to the slaying of 40-year old social worker, Bruce Dahl, in a drug-induced fit of anger at "The Establishment."

...testified that he and he alone killed Dahl and threw the remains of Dahl's body into the Blackfoot River.

...an extravagant story of crime and demonism...under tight security in the Missoula Courthouse. "He was garbage, garbage–and deserved it anyway probably," Sypher said after the court appearance and to a brief gathering of newsmen afterwards...

"I was 'stoned,' but awake when we pitched sleeping bags...when I woke-up again there was lightning and thunder. By then it was done, I think. I'm not too sure of the time..."

...felt bad about the gentleman who discovered the torso. "I'm a trout fisherman myself, and I'm sorry for that event," he said.

Handcuffed...persistent nervous kicking of crossed leg. Led away...

Cole sucked his cheek. "Well, at least I said 'remains' and not 'bits' of body, and I said 'an extravagant' and not 'a horror' story of drugs,

30

and all that sensationalizing. But why did Virgil Sypher say 'he and he alone' did it? And that Dahl deserved it 'anyway probably'? Was he putting us on–about his pyrotechnic trance during the lightning, and his sorriness for that 'gentleman' fisher-folk? Or was he putting himself on?"

"We'll never know it all," Mavis said.

"Still, maybe we can know something. I want you to go over to Butte and talk to some people."

"Oh, no."

"Oh yes. Did Sypher have a violent boyhood, for instance? What are his parents like? Teachers' impressions? Deeper than any of that sob-story stuff we got once or twice at the time."

Ray Unruh came over. "I happened to overhear," he said directly.

"So: you want to go over there, too?"

"I just finished the Society Page. Wilbur, I'm only *pasting*. I'm fed up asking that VRT machine–all right, it's beautiful–it is!–to hyphenate and justify for me, and then I scissor a piece and paste it on the graph-line master sheet."

"You just press it on; we don't paste anymore."

"OK, OK, but let me get out of here for a while–go over there with Mavis–help her."

"All right. Mavis, you take Sypher's mother. Ray, you've got the father. Keep them separate. And then, Mavis, some school teachers–and Ray at their sheriff's office, with more details than what the record shows."

Jaunty, Unruh said, "Let's go, Mave."

"Mave?"

"It's called nicknaming. By association: 'Dave' to 'Mave.' Comradely."

"All right, Wisky."

"Whiskey?"

"It's nicknaming. Also association: for Wisconsin, right?"

Cole looked up and spoke to the overhead light fixture. "Lamp," he intoned, "they may leave."

"Come on," Ray said. "Just call me sweetheart."

He grabbed his jacket and Mavis took her bag, and they left. He was a little short for her, but they looked all right.

* * *

At the State desk, Stoddard said, "Take a letter."

Heinz sat down abruptly at his City desk. "OK."

"No, that's two."

"O."

"That's better. To: R.J. Fleming, Editor. Re: Your Assistant Editor. Re-re: Wilbur Cole's flagrant matchmaking. Namely, assigning Mavis Ridpath and Ray Unruh time-o-sameously to Butte."

32

"How do you spell that? B-e-a-u-t? As in 34 by 28–"

"She's not 28," Stoddard said. "Is Unruh 34? That's getting old."

"Maybe he means Cole," Forbis came into it.

"He's old, alright. Older. Old enough to be a matchmaker."

They all looked at him.

"Never mind the routine." Cole said. "Get to work. This may be the slowest newsroom in the west."

He left in mock irritation.

He stopped at the switchboard and told gum-chewing Sally where he'd be downtown for the balance of the morning; at ex-county Attorney Richard Goheen's and at Julius Grubb's. "Then I'll go home for lunch. On my way back I'll see Judge Barth."

Sally nodded vacantly. She was in the middle of blowing an impressive bubble, which she burst and swallowed back.

Although the town had its California shopping centers, sprawling out to the open landscape on three sides, downtown Missoula was all-compact with lawyers' offices, Courthouse, Post Office, the main clinic and hospital, and the newspaper. You got your fast food and entertainment out on the peripheries, but "Downtown" still had civic meaning to it. Anyway, all the life and death facilities were within walking distance.

Cole went the two blocks or so to Goheen's office. He passed the Cambridge bar, café, and poker room. They had a chalkboard in the window with a special written on it: PIG'S FEET. He didn't know if it was a very old sign or a current one. He went on, heading for Goheen's.

CHAPTER TEN

Dick Goheen was a dark, sharp-faced peppery man. Somewhat self-important, he made you feel that he was losing valuable time. It became clear very quickly that he'd had only two interests in the Sypher case: safe extradition and swift confession. He had gotten both. He'd been shrewd enough to know that it would not have been the kind of case to make a name for himself on–there would be too much unpleasantness stubbornly attached and too much attention on the defendant himself.

"Why is it," Cole asked, "that Sypher was charged with first degree and not second degree murder?"

"Ha," Goheen answered.

"The difference is premeditation, isn't it–?"

"Listen," Goheen cut him short, "even with famous Julius Grubb for the defense, I would have gone ahead and tried him for first and not second degree, if it came to it. And won it."

"All I meant was–"

"Did he do it?" Goheen almost snapped. "Or didn't he?"

"Yes. But–"

"You going to talk about extenuating circumstances?"

"No. I don't think that was the legal point."

Goheen had gone too far. "That's right." He stood up. "Just to be clear–he cannibalized him, didn't he?"

"It certainly looked it. Actually, all you had was his word for it."

34

"Well, the victim was in no condition to give testimony."

"Somebody else *could* have done that."

"Well," Goheen came around his desk toward his door. "I had someone. He seemed convincing enough at the time. And I'm not changing my mind now."

"Thanks," Cole said. "I'm obliged for your time."

"Do you know something, Mr. Cole? Actually, there is no law against cannibalism in this state."

"What?"

"That's right. I don't think, *per se*, there is one in any state."

"I'll be damned."

"Not if you're a cannibal–only if you're a murderer. That's the distinction."

Goheen opened his door.

"But in *effect*," Cole said, "you would have tried him for first-degree cannibalism? Although there is no specific statute for it."

"That's right," Goheen smiled wanly.

They nodded to one another instead of saying good-bye.

* * *

Julius Grubb, on the other hand, welcomed Cole and made him comfortable. In fact, he took him to two armchairs he had away from his desk at the opposite end of his office and sat with him there, easing down into one of the chairs and taking out a cigar. He offered one to Cole, who declined.

"Mr. Grubb, since Virgil Sypher confessed anyway, what did he say about the rest of the victim's body? If it's not violating confidence or privileged relation."

"The man's past privilege."

"You mean, because of what he did?"

"I mean, he's dead and gone."

"He's dead, yes. Not quite gone if–"

"–we're talking about him?" Grubb looked briefly at the ceiling, through it quickly, beyond. "Some Orthodox people believe that every time you talk about the dead, they live again. Or that they get another shove or push into eternity." He shook his great bald head. "I'm not religious, though. Thank God, I don't believe anything much." Then he almost choked on his cigar, laughing at his irreverent reverence. "What was your question again?"

"About the remains."

Grubb puffed out another cloud. The aromatic space between them was getting dim and blue.

"I think he originally said he threw them in the water. Then he said he buried them. Finally he said, 'I don't remember.'"

"To *you* even? Not just to Goheen?"

"Yes, me. Funny thing, I got to believe him. He plain didn't remember–or couldn't allow himself to–but, one way or the other, *didn't*."

"You say, you believed it then. Do you now?"

"Yes."

"Were you ever privately repelled, in the case?"

"I try to make it a practice, Mr. Cole, of not judging. That's what judge and jury are for."

"I was thinking and speaking off the record. I gather you weren't put off by Sypher, personally?"

"No. For the short time I had anything to do with the case, I almost liked him."

They stood up. The blue smoke was all over their part of the room.

"Oh," Cole asked, "Did he say where he got the gun?"

"In all his mis-remembering, or non-remembering, finally, I think he said he got it from maybe 'a box.' I'm not sure."

"Well, thanks, Mr. Grubb."

"My pleasure. What are you going to do with this information?"

"Just follow it on out. See what I come up with, systematically."

"Leave it alone, Mr. Cole."

"Why?"

"I have bad feelings about it. Probably useless premonitions. Anyhow, why not leave the dead alone?"

They walked slowly to the door.

"You're not religious, but you're superstitious?" Cole observed.

Julius Grubb laughed. "That's funny," he acknowledged. "Still, let it be, Mr. Cole."

They shook hands.

"I more or less generally do," Cole said. "This is my exception."

Grubb shrugged. He opened the door. His lit cigar made a flamboyant swirl in the blue smoke, on which he choked. Then, wordlessly, he ushered Cole out.

* * *

District Court Judge Lloyd Barth was youthful, even athletic looking. He was giving Cole a few minutes before resuming a current trial at two o'clock.

"You know, we had pretty tight security for the Sypher arraignments," he said. He seemed proud of that. Unlike Goheen, he had probably wanted a trial.

"Members of Dahl's family?"

"Yes. And some people in general."

"But nothing happened?"

"No." Perhaps he sighed. "As it was, the lynching, if that's what it was, came in the State penitentiary."

"Excuse me, Judge–why did he ever get there? I mean–why wasn't he judged insane and sent to Utah?" Without a prison for the criminally insane of its own, Montana had an agreement with its neighbor, paying Utah on a prorated, or per capita, basis. "After all?"

"Well, as you know, I had a confidential psychiatric report. It certified his competence. Our own people said he could stand trial proceedings."

"But mutilation like that–and cannibalism–didn't all that call for–"

"Mercy?"

"No, sir. I didn't mean that. Wasn't he–to the layman anyway–at least temporarily insane?"

"You could argue that just about everybody is in any violent crime."

"All right, then: permanently, criminally insane."

"It's more difficult to decide than you think. For instance, in our state, did the alleged mental illness or condition *directly* lead to or account for the resultant crime? At the request of counsel, Mr. Grubb, who I hoped would so move, and did, I asked for the psychiatric examinations to so determine. No such mental condition was found."

"But in the terms of everybody around here–deep-down and common-sensibly–wasn't he crazy to do what he did?"

All Judge Barth said was, "I take your meaning–that he'd probably be alive now otherwise."

"That's not my main point."

"It is not on my conscience, however. Everything was quite regular."

Judge Barth put his two hands on his desk and seemed to do a modified push-up in order to stand.

"Thank you, Your Honor."

"You're quite welcome. Good-bye."

"Bye."

CHAPTER ELEVEN

Later that day, on his way home, Cole swung by the university. He wanted a different kind of conversation. He parked at the Health and Science Building and went in the back door to see his friend, Zachary Wyld, professor of Wildlife Management.

He walked downstairs to the cage room. Wyld and his assistant, Ollie Blastic, were feeding three coyotes they had inside.

They watched the animals eat. Zack never kept his captured animals very long, Cole knew that a cage was prison, and they hadn't done anything wrong. Wyld would make observations and measurements and do his doctoring and then release them in some free landscape again.

Cole thanked them for helping Mavis out. Wyld shrugged, meaning it was nothing; but Ollie Blastie rolled his eyes appreciatively.

Cole talked about the Sypher case. "The investigation makes me restless," he said. "I just came from the Judge, who's more interested in clearing himself of any mistake than in strictly recalling the facts or possibilities. Maybe that's all that happens in any interview."

"I appreciate being a friend of yours," Zack Wyld said, "but I'm glad I deal with animals."

They stood looking at the coyotes.

"How far do they travel in a day, Zack?"

"Oh, anywhere up to twenty-five miles. On the average, closer to fifteen."

"By the way, what do you suppose a dog's range is?"

Zack Wyld turned to Ollie Blastic.

"Depends on size," Ollie answered, smiling. "German shepherds go farther than toy poodles."

"An ordinary, average, neighborhood dog?"

"Well, I'd say a mile. Nor more than two."

They stood and talked there a while together. Then Ollie left them alone.

"Answer a question," Cole said.

"Don't I always?"

"No, sometimes you laugh, even if it's not–ho-ho, out loud. Ollie Blastic almost did, about shepherds and poodles. I guess I deserve it sometimes."

"What's on your mind?"

"Is cannibalism rare or not in the animal world?"

"You'll be pointing me to judgment, I just know it."

"Answer up."

"Listen, anything that happens, happens. If it occurs at all, in the balance of nature, it's–natural. Predation is. Even some intra-species predation. Most fish, for instance. A few birds. Some primitive men. That's all."

"Off the record," Cole asked, "don't you have a favorite—depravity, from nature?"

"No–well, yes," Wyld said. "Magpies."

"Magpies?"

"I saw a starving deer once during a bad winter. I was on snowshoes and had just broken into a clearing. The scrawny deer was folded down, too weak to stand anymore. Dying of starvation, collapsing. There was a magpie already pecking her eye."

Both men shuddered.

"You wouldn't put that magpie in a permanent cage?" Cole asked.

"Of course not. It was just scavenging–too fast. Anyway, to show you how far I'm out of it, I'd have killed it first. Why do so many liberals think life imprisonment is better than death?"

"They figure there's maybe some hope for a deer that got drunk on rotting windfall apples or for a coyote that went rabid: the drunk will pass, maybe there'll be a cure-all shot for rabies. And that magpie you saw–it was probably young, it could stand growing up in its feathers."

"You're one of those, all right," Wyld said. He patted Cole's suit coat in bantering mockery. "Say, you've got a bleeding heart. You know the thing about people, Wilbur Cole? We're all the animals together–a little deer in us, some coyote, a magpie, a weasel, a–"

"Zack, you're getting pretty deep."

"It must be your fault. Generally, I make it a habit not to think at all. It's bad for the brain."

Cole glanced around the premises.

"And supposedly, you're some kind of professor," he said.

"Shh, don't tell on me."

Cole clapped him on the back and started off.

"In case you haven't noticed, I'm leaving."

"You're escaping," Wyld said.

"From what?"

"I don't know," Wyld concluded. "Something I said."

CHAPTER TWELVE

The next day Ray Unruh was back. Without Mavis, who had quit.

"She couldn't stand the gaff."

"Give me the gaff," Cole said, at his desk in Fleming's office. "We'll get to Mavis afterwards."

Unruh sat down. He took out his note papers and spread them. He was ready to read and report.

"Shoot," Cole said.

"Please," Unruh held up hands against the word. "Not after Butte! I'm going to have to start packing a rod if I stay with this thing. You know, we saw one high school street fight and one bar-door brawl just on the way back and forth from dinner." Ray straightened his notes.

"Did you see Virgil Sypher's parents?"

"Not exactly. The mother and father were separated some time ago, and then she died. Tim Sypher is living with *his* mother, Virgil's grandmother. I spoke to him in what passes for a living room, and Mavis spoke to her in the kitchen."

"And?"

"I figure he's drunk *all* the time, but less in the morning. But he's 'against drugs'–all right?–'which is the downfall of this country.'" Ray Unruh made quote signs with his fingers. "He was so mad at Virgil's using drugs instead of good hard liquor that he never went to see him even in jail in Missoula."

"What's he do for a living?"

"He's a miner. I don't know how he can tell quartz from gallons, but evidently he still functions down underground. And aboveground he still goes on hunting and fishing trips. By the way, he used to take Virgil and a cousin on some hunts and tried to teach them how to shoot and skin game. Virgil 'warn't much good at it.'"

"At what–shooting or butchering?"

"There was an auto accident when he was sixteen. Car full of teenagers hit a telephone pole on a rainy day. Nobody really hurt, but Virgil's big dumb cousin, Ambrose Johnson, about two years younger, was unconscious by a pool of water near the pole. Virgil went to get him but stepped into that water where there was also a broken high voltage wire, and he got shocked out of his head and burned on the legs. When he came to, he resuscitated his cousin. It was in the papers."

"Anything else–especially of violent interest?"

"No–not in the newspaper files, not in the sheriff's records. Nothing. That's it."

"And the big dumb cousin?"

"Moved away."

"And Virgil, after high school?"

"He wanted to join the Army but was rejected. Get this: he had one gray eye and one brown eye. They can turn you down for that."

"Rejection, rejection. His employment record?"

"Between what the old man and the grandmother knew or got postcards about, we pieced some things together. He tried seriously for rodeo, getting to Denver, but failed. Worked on a dude ranch–the White

46

Tail–up around the Clearwater. Then for a Bitterroot rancher–Arnold Mutch–for a while; some kind of trouble there. Then as a dishwasher in Missoula–a card saying how he hated indoor work. Then as a Libby dam worker. Then in a place called, I think, Shoop's Auto Body, in Missoula again. Then he was either out of work or out of contact, or both. He's our born loser. That's it."

"What happened to you and Mavis?"

Unruh stared at him. Then he shuffled his notes together.

"No transition?" he asked.

"What spooked Mavis?"

"I think it started with the Frankenstein part, the electricity thing. Or maybe the Sypher house: Tim Sypher, in sleeveless undershirt, and his red eyes barely open at you, and beer cans all over the living room. And those street fights she saw."

Cole nodded. "And your contribution?"

"All right, for some goddamn reason, I made sick jokes. 'You notice the jar of ashes they had on the mantel? The mother was cremated. Every morning they have a cup of Instant Mama for breakfast.' That turned her off–and some others. And next morning, out loud, driving out of Butte, noticed a steam shovel ripping up a pit, like jaws chewing the earth. I was being profound, but she thought I was still telling sick jokes."

"So she looked out her window all the way back."

"Right. Got out of the car at her place in Missoula, slammed the door, and said she was through–with me, the job, everything."

"Making you my sole legman now, my exclusive assistant in this review."

"Hey, wait a second a minute!–"

"OK. I take that back. Anyway I'll call her–or she'll call me or she'll just show up again. But whatever happens, don't *you* call her just now–or mention anything later."

Unruh nodded sagaciously. He picked up his note papers and left.

CHAPTER THIRTEEN

Cole was on the phone again with Robert Sculli.

Sculli said, "Never mind Unruh–and his steam shovel erosions: by the way, like violating Mother Earth. It's you I want to talk about. What's your motive, finally? And don't dwell on past inefficiency and all that."

"Deep down, I want to know the worst possible scenario."

Cole's brave moment lasted only the pause it took Sculli to reply. "No. That's only half- depth."

"What is it then, since you're going to tell me anyway?"

"Similar to repetition compulsion–we return to something, which we were not really able to absorb, to try again."

"I wasn't able to assimilate it fully? I'm trying–once more–to take the measure of what is, for me anyway, unimaginable evil? OK. Maybe there's a time for everybody–later than we thought–when we can get to the bottom of something like depravity. *Now,* for some reason, is my time. That's what makes it feel urgent, I guess."

Sculli sighed into his phone. Cole pictured him grimacing.

"That's only part of it–as the first thing that comes eagerly into someone's head is usually only half of it. Wilbur, Wilbur: you *don't* want to find out what you say you do. You're one of those good Americans, don't you know, who want to find out the opposite. Deep down–though you harden yourself on the surface and throw out remarks about 'butchering' and all that–*deep* down you want to discover redeeming features in the most terrible story that's happened here. You want to find out that it wasn't *all* bad. I hope the whole thing doesn't turn *actually* dangerous."

"Which it already is, psychologically?"

There was a pause.

"I think you'll come out all right. Still, take care, Wilbur, and–"

"What?"

"Don't go too far on this whole thing."

"How far is that?"

"Who knows?" Sculli asked. "Who ever knows?"

* * *

Cole was in Spahn's office. In the Helena packet were the knife, sealed in a clear plastic envelope, and bits of dark green plastic also in a clear envelope. Also mugshots of Sypher and sheets of his fingerprints.

"Raise your right hand," Sheriff Spahn said.

"What?"

"Come in here, Milly," Spahn called in his secretary as a witness. He was not fooling. "Keep that arm up. I'm going to deputize you."

"Why?"

"For two reasons. To handle evidence–even in a past case. Actually, I'm not sure of that, but I think so. But I'm sure of the second reason."

"Which is what?"

"To handle evidence in a present case. Also if this whole thing takes a sudden turn."

"Like what?"

Spahn looked at him. "I don't rightly know. Anyhow, just do it."

Sheriff Spahn administered and Wilbur Cole took the oath.

"Thank you, Milly. All right now, here's the knife."

"Can I just send a man over from the paper for a picture of it? Then we can enlarge it and make a duplication for an idea of mine."

"OK. By the way, Sypher's prints are on the knife, of course. That's what these here pictures are."

"Still, can we check for *other* prints?"

"Like for an original housewife owner? Or a print we just couldn't trace anyhow?"

"Well, you never know what'll come through."

"Hey!" Spahn laughed. "Who's the sheriff around here?"

"But I'm a deputy, remember?" He clapped Spahn on the back. "Listen, can I have this mug shot for a while?"

"Sure."

Cole picked up the envelope with the dark plastic bits in it. He studied it.

"No," Spahn said, "they're too tiny for getting prints."

"Then can I feel a piece?"

"Open it up."

Cole did so and took out and felt a piece, gingerly. "It's too thin for 6-mil outdoor stuff."

"Ground cover, for tents?"

"I don't think so." Cole put it back in the envelope. "Well, I'll send a man over to photograph the knife, and I'll get this mug shot back to you."

"No hurry."

Cole looked at him pleasantly and said, "I know." But he felt urgent.

CHAPTER FOURTEEN

In the newsroom, Cole passed by Unruh's desk just as Ray popped another dry aspirin.

"Here's another possible headache for you. Mavis is back," Cole said, indicating Mavis, who sat waiting at Cole's desk. "To *me*, she never quit; just an indisposition that day."

"Sure," Ray said.

"Come on, I've got more assignments on the thing for the both of you."

At his desk Cole said, "Mavis, get some more background on Bruce Dahl, from his co-workers especially. Also–" he handed her a series of enlarged photos that *Tribune* photographer, Carl Atkins, had made– "don't jump–look at these."

Mavis took the photos. They were four different views of the knife and then two more blown-up concentrations on handles and blade.

"It's the handle you'll be especially interested in." That was not only because Cole wanted to distract her from the confounding of blood and rust on the blade, but because of the illegible name on the handle. "That's certainly an 'S' for the start of the manufacturer's name, but the rest is unclear. Still, somebody at some restaurant you're going to may find that helpful in recognizing it."

"And if I can manage coming up with a cook or owner who says, 'Oh yeah, that was when Virgil Sypher was here too,' you'd like that."

"Short of fantasy, do what you can."

"Girl Scouts' honor and 4-H," she said brightly. "You can't beat that."

"Sounds healthy," Unruh said, trying to grace himself in, "but is it reliable?"

"As for you," Cole said, "go up the Clearwater today and visit the White Tail Dude Ranch. Tomorrow, go the opposite way, to Arnold Mutch's ranch on the Bitterroot."

"'Good, good!' he ejaculated—now there's a slip of the tongue." Unruh was marking his note pad and looked up, pleased with himself.

"Ray," Cole said, "how many times have I told you not to talk when your mouth is open?"

Mavis said, "I was leaving anyway. Bye!" she sang back.

Unruh turned to go, too.

"Listen," Cole advised him, "don't crack wise with the ranch people."

Ray waved his assent and left.

Cole went downstairs, looking for Carl Atkins.

"You see this?" he showed Carl the mug shot of Sypher.

"You want that enlarged, too?"

"Yes. And something else a little out of your line–except that I've just made you staff artist."

"Any increase in salary?"

"No. Sorry."

"I'm sorry, too. I decline the honor."

"It's not exactly an honor, it's what everybody likes to do for a practical joke sometime. Put whiskers on this mug shot after you blow it up to, say five by seven?"

"Sure. Doesn't sound like a joke. Sounds like imagination."

Cole laughed.

"Remind me to put you in for a promotion."

"Just get me the money," Atkins said.

CHAPTER FIFTEEN

Cole was in the office of Harold Reynolds, manager of the State Employment Service in Missoula. Reynolds stood at an open file cabinet, leaning on it as he flipped through a folder for Cole's benefit. He was a quick-moving man with slender pianist's hands, which, in fact, played deftly over several typed sheets and some blank white paper as if they were wide keys.

"White Tail Ranch–Mutch–Brock's Place–Libby Dam–Shoop Auto–Unemployment insurance…"

"Yes," Cole said. "A reporter of mine checked on the ranches a few days ago. Nothing on the White Tail Dude Ranch, except maybe he couldn't stand the dudes. But there was a dispute at Arnold Mutch's working ranch."

"Yes. Mr. Mutch–" Harold Reynolds leaned over to the door, and tipped it closed. "–has consistently paid his hay balers below minimum wage."

"So you went after him?"

"No. We *must* have a signed complaint. Sypher evidently came down here, like a dozen others, complained–but didn't sign."

"Why is that?"

"They think it'll wind up in a court, or simply get more and more complicated. Probably they begin feeling guilty. Instead of the other party!"

"The system seems wrong."

"It is." Reynolds made a delicate snorting noise. "We just administer it."

"Well, thanks. Oh, I take it that his unemployment insurance finally ran out?"

Reynolds' fingers turned–then struck a note. "Yes, indeed."

"And one other thing–what was that entry between Arnold Mutch and Libby Dam?"

Reynolds found it. "Brock's."

"Brock's what?"

"It says, 'Hole-in-the-Wall,'" Reynolds read. "I think it must be–"

"–a café on Woody Street, by the railroad tracks. I've seen it. Any dispute or unpleasantness there?"

"Just a notation later by our interviewer that 'employee can't stand indoor work.' Not very serious."

"It was a life, Mr. Reynolds. That's serious."

"Not this one," Reynolds said, decisively closing up the folder. In fact, he put the folder back in place in the file drawer and then slammed the drawer in, making Cole think of an actual sliding morgue portal.

Cole looked at him steadily for two or three seconds. "Thanks anyway," he said.

He went out.

Of course Brock might or might not remember, even from a picture. Or he might have sold out by now, or closed down. Social instability:

rampant. But Cole would leave a note for Mavis at the *Tribune*. It was worth the chance.

* * *

On the phone to Sculli, Cole said:

"Here's another Freudian slip for you, Robert. There was off-color repartee in the newsroom, and Mavis was coming over, and Ray said, 'Hold it–babies present.' That's right, not 'ladies' but 'babies'...Mavis? She picked up something from her desk, patted Ray and said, just as sweet as can be, 'Rest in peace.' Not 'Drop dead,' more elevated. Yes, she was the lady just then. I gave her the bearded photo that Atkins made for us to carry around to some restaurants, one in particular. And I put Ray on the North Side, to knock on doors just in case somebody is still there who saw or knew the dog with the outsized bone. Me? I'm stopping by at the Bonner mill and then going fishing up the Blackfoot. Yes, at the crime site this time. You're not invited, just me and–ghosts."

* * *

Gary Stetson, work foreman at the Bonner mill, was a youngish, serious man. He wore a dress shirt and tie, but he folded back his wide, stiff cuffs almost to his elbows.

"Sypher's record had just too many firings and quittings. And no references," he said.

"So you turned him down. Any unpleasantness?"

Stetson shook his head.

"Not unless you mean that–Sypher just stared at me. He didn't shout or wave arms or threaten in any way. Just stared a long time. Then turned around and left. Sort of bolted out of the place."

Bolted up the twisty road, like his future, ahead of him. Cole, thanking Stetson and driving on up the Blackfoot, thought of Sypher's fated, unskilled, continuously balked non-career. Cole passed MacIlhaney's Bar, drove along the canyon road past the regular state campsite. Along this same stretch, walking and thinking, Sypher may have felt a dull, rising hysteria in him, still needing triggering.

Cole pulled off the road and eased into the other area. He stopped the car, got out.

Eyes averted from the wooded scene, he carefully put together his gear. Then he walked back downstream quickly along the shore in order to fish first and come up gradually from below.

* * *

Eventually, Cole worked his way upstream. He fished the end of an oxbow. Then he went in to shore. He walked up to the flat area amid the trees. Right there. He sat on a fallen rotting log and stared about him. The demented buzz of an overheated autumn horsefly distracted him but then it whined and swirled off, crazing through the trees.

There was a lull on the highway just now, soundlessness. Cole stared fixedly, a late witness. Was he hypnotized? Self-hypnotized? He looked slowly, objectively, from his left to his right and back again, all around.

In a way, was Sypher, too, only a witness–to his own hypnotized self doing the crime? Wait a minute, back up (Cole, in fact, sat back on his fallen log, from which he had slid forward too far): *was* there lightning and thunder that night? But it doesn't matter what there actually was, Sculli has always said, only what somebody thought there was–because *that's* his reality.

Cole heard the sound of water, reassuring, and then a crackling sound, unexpected. He started, even stood up. Late drying caragana pods were splitting apart, popping. Relieved, he shuffled about in the clearing.

He inspected a tree where, in fact, he found a sort of narrow, sap-filled scar. He touched the place. Was this where the knife blade was stuck? Don't trees bleed, too?

Cole gripped his rod and headed for his car, down a little distance. He knew he'd be back here–once more, in his full imagination of what happened. But he wanted to leave now.

There was an after-image, as he walked to the car, of the late sun-speckledness in the dense grove of the place behind. It stayed in his eye and on his mind–baffled tree-light, and a whole, settling dark.

CHAPTER SIXTEEN

Cole sat at his newsroom desk, where a shaft of sunlight came in from a nearby window. Sally came over, holding two note papers in her hand.

"Mavis Ridpath left a message," she said, and then read one note to Cole: "'No luck at Brock's Place. But he said there's Solingen knifeware at the Flowers Hotel. Will check–half-heartedly.'"

"Is that a pun?" Cole asked.

"What?"

"Never mind, it's just me. What was the other?"

"Oh." Sally read the other note. "'Called the Weather Bureau for that night of June 26. There was no lightning. But there may have been northern lights visible that night.'"

"OK. Thanks. When you get back to the switchboard, will you try for Deputy–" Cole had to consult a slip of his own– "Hal Long at the Sacramento, California, State Police Headquarters?"

Sally nodded and left. Cole laced his hands behind his head, swiveled and stared out the sunny window.

"You know," Stoddard said from the State Desk, "I'm pretty sure I remember Grandma Sypher at the time of Virgil's capture saying, 'Nothing like this ever happened to us before.'"

"You're making it up," Heinz said.

Forbis said, "No, I know him. He hasn't got the imagination."

"Listen to the bores," Stoddard said, maybe to Cole. "The bland leading the bland."

Cole's phone rang. He swiveled back to get it.

"Officer Long? Missoula, Montana. Cole of the *Tribune*–re-working the Virgil Sypher case. You remember that arrest? Never will forget it? Of course. Listen, about the car–I mean the interior. Was there, well, blood in the trunk? No? And in the interior of the car? Oh. You recall *some*thing on the passenger's floorboard. Blood type later confirmed as victim's. He simply might have cut himself on that side once. So, no killing, at any rate, in the car. Right. Well, thanks again, very much. Bye."

Cole hung up, just as Ray Unruh came in. Ray looked slightly bedraggled but pleased with himself. Still, he stopped at his own desk first, where he took one or two aspirin from his aspirin box, and then he came over and plunked down in the chair beside Cole's desk.

"How's your fishing lately?" he asked.

"Nothing doing the last time out," Cole said.

"Not even with the special fly I give you?"

"No. Never mind the small talk, how goes it?"

"Almost dangerous, sometimes. Do you know that when I interviewed Arnold Mutch in one of his fields, he was on a tractor and had a shotgun along under the seat? He made a little move to it when my questions got uncomfortable. I'm not going to send *him* a Christmas card."

Cole suppressed a smile. "How's your North Side exploration going?"

"Also a hassle and a half. But I like it, too. Especially when I get brainstorms."

"Like what?"

"Like noticing the North Side Bar—and just going *there* finally."

"And asking the bartender, who knows everything and everybody in the neighborhood."

"Not this one, he's new. But he remembered that the boss remembered or knew something. It's a lead. I'll go back tonight."

"Good. I may go over with you."

Ray got up, just as Cole's phone rang again. Cole picked it up; he made a stop sign of his fanned hand, for Ray to wait.

"It's Mavis—she's got something."

Ray's face fell a little.

"The Flowers Hotel?" Cole listened to Mavis. "The kitchen—you showed the chef the knife picture. It was made back east—Sheboygan, not Solingen. So: it was a Missoula-owned knife, and not necessarily stolen, maybe just slid into refuse and later recovered—and turning up on the Blackfoot. Good. Concentrate on Dahl now. Incidentally, Ray has a lead on the North Side dog. OK." He hung up. He said to Ray, "She says, here's hoping."

"I'll drink to that," Ray said.

CHAPTER SEVENTEEN

It was evening. They were driving to the North Side Bar through a network of winding and looped streets in that part of town. Cole was at the wheel.

"I think we're on the right street," Ray Unruh said. "A block before you get to Nordstrom Plywood, turn left."

"How the hell—"

Unruh was already shaking his head against himself. "I know how that sounded, but in the daytime you can see Nordstrom's, like a big gym roof. It was my marker. But at night, you can't make it out, and Ray the Unruh sounds weird."

"Actually, it was funny," Cole said. Also marvelously self-centered. "There it is."

He pulled up to the bar. It had a staccato or nervous neon sign outside its window. Cole locked the car, and they went in.

The man behind the bar was a thick-set man of medium height. He moved and talked very deliberately. Unruh had elbowed Cole when they came in to indicate that this was not the afternoon bartender, but probably the owner.

Cole ordered a beer and Unruh a Boilermaker—because the *Tribune* or Cole was paying?—and they introduced themselves. It was shortly after supper and there was only one other customer at the far bend of the bar looking abstractedly at the TV hung in the corner there.

"Chester Graves," the owner said. Cole motioned to him to take something himself. "I don't allow my barkeeps or myself to do that," Graves said. He was perfectly serious. You might say, sober.
64

Cole let Unruh recall the cannibal story. Graves was impassive. Unruh got to the dog. Graves, who had been slouching on the bar, stood up straight.

"Oh yeah," he remembered something. "I knew that dog. He was, he was–"

Cole and Unruh both stiffened, inclining their heads toward Graves now, as if to help him mesmerically picture that dog again.

"Bastard," Graves said. But he was not swearing. "He was a mixed breed, half-terrier and half-lab. Funny looking. But all right. He's dead now."

Cole subsided in his seat, and Ray downed his shot and relapsed next to this beer.

"Whose was it?"

"Dunno. Somebody, somebody–"

"Who, Chet?" Unruh asked. "Who?"

"Chester," Graves said, "not Chet. I'm not ever Chet."

Cole was shaking his head. Ray's quick, inappropriate intensity threatened the mood; he said, "Sorry" and took a contrite gulp of beer.

Cole addressed Graves softly. "How do you know the dog's dead, for sure?"

"He's dead," Graves answered "Car accident or something."

"Oh."

"Wait a minute–I just remembered who owned that dog. Big dumb guy...named...Johnson–"

Unruh swallowed the wrong way. Choked.

"–which I don't see him anymore," Graves said. "Not for years even. He used to come in here, a lot, but no more. Maybe left, after his brother or cousin."

Cole looked at Unruh, who had recovered, then back to Graves. "Was the name, Ambrose Johnson?"

"Yeah, that was the whole name."

"And the man who brought him in here, bought him the dog probably, took care of him: Virgil Sypher?"

Graves shook his head. "Never heard of him."

"But–" Ray started out. He felt Wilbur Cole's cautionary hand on his arm.

"Thanks," Cole said.

Graves left for another customer.

"I'm going home," Cole said to Ray, "Leave Chester alone now."

"But–"

"I'll put Mavis on the Johnson lead tomorrow and get that Sypher blow-up from her, and we'll come back here tomorrow night. Understand?"

"OK."

Cole stood, about to go. He reached over to a saucer of dried jerky chips and slid it over in front of Ray.

"You can eat beef jerky," he said. "That's your business. Just stay away from any tongue."

66

Unruh understood.

* * *

At his newsroom desk the next day, Cole scrutinized some sheets he held. Mavis stood behind him, peering over his shoulder.

"I like this report of yours on Dahl. Well-written."

He re-read the first paragraph aloud.

"'Bruce Dahl was, from all indications, a finicky 40-year-old bachelor probably misplaced in his line of work. He had been doing social service work in Missoula for just under a year, but the more perceptive of his co-workers believe he was perhaps more suited to bureaucratic clerical work than to hands-on social caseloads. His attitude was mechanical, uncommitted and probably unsympathetic.'"

Cole glanced up. "As a matter of fact, Mavis, it's a little too well-written, with too high a vocabulary. But I like its substance." He returned to the report, excerpting it.

"'His manner with clients was falsely hearty and optimistic. He gave a good, helpful first impression. But he had a 'low rate of resolutions,' according to one source. Once he was pummeled in his office by a client.'"

"'As a schoolboy in Livingston, Dahl carried the flag for some parades and ballgames. He never participated in any sports. His parents did own a registered .32 revolver. They never reported it missing, but it was. Undoubtedly the victim took it, since he had said once or twice in Missoula that, 'like everybody else,' he now had a 'piece' for self-defense. The 'box' that Virgil Sypher remembered at one point where he may have found or seen the gun could be Dahl's glove compartment…Dahl…killed at midnight, according to the Coroner. He had, therefore, conversed probably for 2-3 hours with Sypher, giving long enough, sufficiently mixed-up provocation."

Cole laid down the report.

"OK. I can't use this as an article, Mavis, least of all at this date. But, like the coyote piece, it was a good exercise. Simplify your style a little and you'll be fine. Anyway, you're off knives and guns, and I'll take the touched-up Sypher picture back, and I want you on this name: Ambrose Johnson. Does he, or did he, have a driver's license, or a Missoula telephone number or address?"

"Ambrose J–"

"That's right, Sypher's cousin. Lived *here*, in town, some years back. Probably with Virgil."

"What a break!"

"Maybe. Just get out there, use your street time on Johnson."

"Any particular hurry?"

"Oh no," Cole said, smiling, "I never say that. I just say do it, starting now."

* * *

Back at the North Side Bar, after supper, Cole ordered a beer and Unruh his boilermaker.

Graves brought them their drinks.

Cole took out the picture. "Recognize this man?"

"Can't say that I–hold it!–that's–that's–"

Ray Unruh blurted, "Virgil–"

Cole glared at Unruh.

"Who?"

"Maybe he had more or less beard than this, some time ago," Cole suggested.

"I know him. I remember now. That's–Sy. He's Ambie Johnson's relative. Sure."

"Sy. Just...Sy? Not Virgil or Sypher?"

"That's all I knew him by."

Chester Graves went off, served another customer, and then came back.

"He came in here, with big ol' Ambie, on and off, maybe for two-three years. Then I never saw 'em again."

"So they lived in the neighborhood then?"

"It figures. But I don't happen to know everybody's whole name and where they exactly live or what they do. Them two used to come on Sunday afternoons, after football season, and catch the old horror movies on the Denver channel."

Graves moved away to serve another customer, then returned. "And Sy finally picked up a girl. Name of–"

Cole shot Unruh a look not to disrupt Graves.

"Joyce," Graves remembered finally. "She don't come in here anymore either."

More people entered the bar. Cole and then Ray Unruh rose to go. They thanked him and said good-bye.

Outside, Cole said, "OK, Mavis has Johnson. You've got Joyce, if you can still find her, like tomorrow."

"Sure. Want to see what another atmospheric bar is like meanwhile?" Unruh suggested. "The night is young."

"Well, I'm not. And, besides, my wife gets edgy if I'm out two nights in a row."

"Man sounds hen-pecked."

"No. This man has got a nice hen, though. Happy hunting, Ray."

"Oh, I already got a floozy...Remember that fly I gave you? I call it the 'royal Cunnilingus: clippings from the nether parts.'"

"What?" Cole stared at Ray Unruh. "You raided–cannibalized–her pudendum for a dry fly?!"

"She didn't mind, even thought it was fun. It didn't work, evidently– but what's the harm otherwise?"

Cole shook his head. "I'm just out of it, nowadays," he said, still shaking his head in the dark. "Just out of it."

CHAPTER EIGHTEEN

On an evening several days later Robert Sculli was at the Coles' house. They sat comfortably at a chess table preparatory to a game. The board was not yet set.

"Remember," Cole said, "I win the games at my house. Sorry Marge couldn't come along."

"Feeling tired. But I'm ready for action." Sculli tugged his earlobe, willing to talk a while before they played. "What was the last thing you called me about in the Sypher matter?"

"That he was not called Sypher. He called himself Sy."

"Ah."

"Nicknames and code names," Cole said. "One of my earliest thoughts was that Sypher spelled another way is zero."

"Unlike a whole school of psychiatrists, I generally dismiss instant Rorschach tests and–I've said this before–the *first* thing that comes into mind. Because it quickly and conveniently hides the *other* thing. In this case, his first name."

"He wanted to avoid–Virgil?"

"Think about it."

"The sound? Virgil–Vir–Virgin. Oh, no."

"Why not?"

"All right, he maybe had some psycho-sexual problems."

"Of course. From my point of view, perfectly predictable. He dissociated or split himself in name as well as fact."

"Fact?" Cole asked.

"The fact of the *crime*, Wilbur. Cannibalism, we've pretty much decided, is a highly schizoid act, among other things. It's a double act, recall. Your savage man kills the horde father or his prized enemy and wants to devour or incorporate what he's destroyed. It's a contradictory or double act. The little innocent or suckling babe wishes to devour whole, sometimes, what he's being nourished by. Our civilized and sacred Eucharist deals with spiritual blood and flesh taken into our bodies. We're all a little dissociated or split, criminals only more so."

Cole thought about it. "Robert, would you have taken him on as a patient?" Sculli nodded. "But wasn't he one of these 'bad' sick ones you once said that you threw out of the office every once in a while?"

"Only if they're malingerers, lying to me."

Cole began setting up chess pieces. He halted.

"But if people are a little split and contradictory by definition–and liars, often to themselves–why do you throw out *certain* selected liars and not others? How do you know the difference?"

"I think I know," Sculli said. "Maybe someday I won't throw anybody out. Meanwhile, I show that *I'm* two men, myself, still trying to be integrated. I'm like everybody else–neurotic and healthy. Like you."

"I shouldn't ask, but–how?"

Sculli took a breath and then proceeded. "Ray Unruh and Mavis Ridpath are real enough persons, I know that, but they also represent two sides of your psyche. He's masculine–competitive. She's not so compulsive. He needs to succeed in this venture, almost at any cost–"

"Well, he needs some credits–he even wants a by-line sometime–because he really wants to move on to Spokane, Seattle, San Francisco, the big world."

"You–or he–can rationalize it like that, but it's also an inner drive. Meanwhile, her nature is more inherently cooperative and, in the end, she can accept failure."

"How does this reflect me exactly?"

"You tend to send Unruh out and around more than her–cars, more extrovert action. She's more statically employed–landscape and/or rooms, absorption. Correct?"

Cole was struck. His elbow inadvertently knocked over the king he had set up.

"Remind me not to tell you too much–you go too far on it."

"It's just a variation on your character: not only masculine and feminine components, but cynical and naïve at the same time, experienced and innocent. In the latter senses, your special American-ness."

"Very interesting. Brilliant maybe."

"*Maybe?!*" Sculli asked or exclaimed. "Only an ex-Nieman Fellow at Harvard can get away with that." They prepared to play. "Anyway, now watch out!"

CHAPTER NINETEEN

Cole was holding a council-of-war in back of the newsroom. At the back wall, in fact. He had gotten Carl Atkins to enlarge a little phone company street map of the city, and they stuck the enlargement up on the wall. Using a pencil on a string, Cole had Ray Unruh draw two concentric circles while Mavis held the center. She held it at an arbitrary point a block or so from the North Side Bar, while Unruh described a circle with a one-mile radius and a second with a two-mile radius. Afterwards they stood away from the wall, with City, State, and Western editorial reinforcement, studying the map.

"Now, where in either area did the dog find that bone?" Cole asked.

"All we have to do," Ray said, "is have a backhoe dig about three feet deep all around these circles. Take about twelve years."

Fred Heinz said, "Those are just the limits of the case–the garbage dump north, Vandiver's Plywood factory west, the B and N tracks south, and Randolph School east. It's everything between and in the middle–$PiR2$ or something."

"So," Stoddard added, "you need a mathematician too, plus a crew of 682,000 old-time coolies."

"It's ridiculous," Forbes said. "Unless you figure exactly where he *had* to go." He approached the map. "Here," he pointed, "the morbid sonofabitch went here. The North Side Cemetery. He buried the bones in a previous grave. Pretty devious, eh?"

"Why?" Mavis asked.

"Don't encourage him," Cole said.

"Because it's the *last* place you'd look."

Heinz said, "You're not going to dig up every gravesite. Besides, why do you even want the missing remains?"

"We don't," Cole answered, "not particularly. We want the place, for another lead. For instance, if that's the place, maybe a cemetery guard knew him."

"Or he slipped into Vandiver's Plywood or Nordstrom's Wood Products and incinerated everything," Heinz speculated. "It's still hopeless."

They sidled away. Cole stayed a moment longer.

"Thank you, lady and gentlemen. You've been no help at all."

"Don't you call *me* gentleman," Unruh said.

Everybody but Unruh settled back at his desk. Ray was on his way out, still on the trail of the girl Joyce.

"Joyce Dayley," he told Cole. "Chester finally remembered her last name."

"You're getting to be a regular customer?"

"Maybe. Anyway I'm getting to know that whole side of town as well as I used to know my way around the U."

"By the way, who's the paleontologist at the university?"

"Madsen," Unruh said after a moment. "Not Matson in chemistry, whose class I was unfortunately in; if he made TNT, it would come out Orange and Pekoe. You want Eric Madsen. Bye!"

Cole chuckled, watching Ray leave, and spoke for the rest to hear. "He's annoying and hostile in certain ways, but he's funny."

Fred Heinz said, "There are good funnies and bad funnies."

"Like good sicks and bad sicks?"

"What?"

"Never mind." Cole had felt a certain coolness just before the council-of-war, between the others and Unruh. "What happened before I came in with that map?" He looked at Mavis.

She said, "They were talking about a new little sweet shop on West Main–"

Stoddard said, "Unruh said they had Bottomless Waiters over there."

"Oh?"

Then Forbis mimicked Unruh, "Actually, they're quadriplegics and they move around on those little rollers.' All right?"

Stoddard said, "He is getting to be a sicknik, Will. Land him a job quick–out of here."

"I've just written to Frank Osborn at the *Boise Times*."

"How about the *Meninger Institute Weekly*?" Forbis said.

"How do you spell that last word?" Heinz asked.

Cole wanted to be fair. "Still, he's the one who got our Johnson lead."

"Good, tell him Johnson's in Kansas City."

Cole's phone rang. He sat down, ending the talk, and took the call.

It was Sheriff Spahn. "We found another print on that knife."

"Oh."

"You have an idea on it?"

"I've got two ideas. Either we try to match it to three or four years of kitchen helpers at the Flowers Hotel–"

"What's your other idea?"

"Ambrose Johnson."

"Who's he?"

"Sypher's close cousin. My guess is he doesn't have any kind of record."

"Then the print's untraceable? Useless."

"Not if we happen to locate Johnson."

"And then match prints? But even then, so what? Accumulating circumstantial evidence. Anything else?"

"That North Side dog, remember? It was Ambie Johnson's."

Spahn whistled in the phone, piercing Cole's ear. "Hey, you're doing fine. I think I'll give you a badge."

"Just your moral support. And lab help."

"Oh, I almost forgot," Spahn said. "They rechecked the knife otherwise and found blood, rust, pine sap and–they think–throw-up. We'll send it to Pathology, in Great Falls, to corroborate?"

"Whatever you think. And Sheriff?–"

"What?"

"Thanks. You're something else."

"That's what you say. I've been called *every*thing; there isn't something else."

"How's this?–you're a peach. Bye."

After he hung up, Cole caught Mavis Ridpath's eye. She came over. He said, "Keep on the Johnson thing. I think we have his print on the knife."

"I've been on it. He never had a license. No phone listing either. By the way, I checked Virgil's address. On his Employment Service and Food Stamp papers it was always 01 North Street; he played games with them–my idea was no help. But I'll stick with it some more."

"One other thing, Mavis. Call up Libby, Montana, sometime–the banks. And here in town, too–find out how he endorsed his cheeks. A minor point, but I want to know."

"OK, Chief."

"I'm not a chief, I don't own a headdress. Anyhow, I'm not wise enough."

"Oh, I don't know," Heinz broke in. "You posted that map. It'll keep us occupied and shut us up for a while. You're pretty shrewd."

"And modest," Stoddard said.

"And he's a man of many parts," Forbis added, looking meaningfully at his two colleagues.

Cole got up and did a quick hands-in-pocket two-step shuffle. "Aw, shucks," he said.

"Question is–" Stoddard began the quip.

"–are they all connected?" Forbis ended it.

"I'm getting out of here," Cole said.

* * *

Cole walked back through the newsroom again. On the rear wall he studied the big map. The Orange Street underpass was the North Side's access to the Interstate. Was Sypher coming in or going out when he stopped at the PayLess station? What difference did it make? Nothing proved anything. All along nothing kept on not proving anything, and yet the non-development seemed to be developing. Cole concentrated harder. He gauged that the PayLess station was halfway between the Missoula Disposal dump yards on that penciled outer circle, west, and the eastern city limits on the right side of the map, but that only meant to him that the station was simply the last opportunity for gas in or around Missoula.

As he turned from the map, Cole had an idea that flared and went out so fast that he could not be sure he had had anything. Or, as in everything else so far, it was more like a synoptic convergence of either near-thoughts or self-deceptions that suggested–he did not know what. He had lost it. He walked away.

He stopped at the switchboard. Sally had no message from either Mavis or Ray. Sheriff Spahn was sending something over for him, though.

"If it's a detailed pathologist's report, tell him no thanks."

"What's a pathologist?" Sally asked. She chewed her gum rapidly and opened her eyes wide. Then she blew a pink bubble and popped it against the roof of her mouth.

Cole said, "Do you realize you're chewing your tongue by substitution?"

"I'm *just* chewing gum."

"That's what they all say," Cole said, smiling, and left.

CHAPTER TWENTY

Cole suddenly decided, as he drove under the Interstate, to turn onto it. He took it down to Orange Street and swung off, and came under the underpass and saw the PayLess station and pulled into it and got some gas. It was mid-afternoon, with one of those limpid early October Montana skies, high with some wisps of cloud in rose-swirls to the west, heartbreakingly tender.

Cole turned from the horizon and had the oil checked. The attendant was not George Langley, the man who had last seen Sypher that night. But would there have been anything further that Langley could have added a couple of years later?

Cole drove off. He started to tour haphazardly, atmospherically maybe, through the North Side of town. He saw the domed roof of the Nordstrom's wood products plant and turned left, to drive through streets of town he had not seen in a dog's age and other streets he had never really known. Near a school he drove through a Speed Zone, which meant slow zone–the world frequently working by opposites. Cole was driving slowly anyway, through the whole area, casually moseying around. He noted another bar, the Northern Pacific Lounge, and passed it.

Turning at the next corner, out of sight of the bar, he stopped suddenly. Did that VW parked in front of the bar have an ID sticker on the left side of the back bumper that said University of Montana Campus Parking? Not that Cole had quickly and subliminally read it just now but rather remembered such a patch on Unruh's car. Cole went on down to the end of the block, turned right, came all the way around the block and then up the street of the bar again and halted behind the Volkswagen. It was Unruh's all right.

The bar was on a corner. To the left, across the intersection, were two huge white birch trees, shadowy and protective even without most of their leaves. Cole drove up and turned left and then swiftly backed around at the free curb under those trees. He switched off the engine and waited.

There was an unused door, he could see, on this side of the bar, too. Over the lintel, he made out: *Ladies' Enterance*. It had been years since the Northern Pacific railway was bought by and merged into the Burlington Northern. Yet there was the old railroad sign hanging down and the hoary misspelling (after the only correctly positioned apostrophe like that he had ever seen) on the nailed or bolted side door.

With nothing else to notice, Cole settled into dull-headed viewing. I'm skulking into myself, he thought, "on the lookout." Exactly why? I want to see what he comes out with. You mean, who. I mean, Joyce Dayley. She changed bars, he figured that out. Good for him. Everything under control. Self-control. How much self? How many nights has he already known her? What's my point, staking out here–to see how familiar he already is with her, when they come out together? *If* they come out together, and they zoom off and you follow–to his place, her place, or a motel. Wilbur, you're a downright living cliché like this.

Cole drove off, gunning the engine somewhat. He headed for the university.

* * *

Eric Madsen, the professor of paleontology, was more than willing to talk. They stood in a display area, with glass cages all in a row.

"Skeletal bones used as clubs," Professor Madsen said, pointing to one case. "Skull remnants, called 'caps,' used as bowls. Ten-inch stone cleavers to sever thighs." Cole turned partly away. "Facts, Mr. Cole. Merely facts."

They walked down the display aisle.

Cole asked, "They don't bother you, sometimes?"

"Why, no."

"They bother me a little," Cole said, "even if they're ancient history."

"I see," Madsen said. "It's pre-history actually."

"Oh yes. Then how do you know for sure about–say, skull cap bowls?"

They halted.

"We know," Madsen said. "There are ways. Corroborations, over and over." He nodded to his own words. "We find out what happened, often how, approximately when, always where. Never, of course, who."

"And the why?"

They resumed walking.

"This is anthropology, not the philosophy department," Professor Madsen observed.

"Right. In a way, then, you're sort of detective and reporter both, after the fact."

"You might put it that way. And, yes, I admit distance protects us from the spectacle of human outrage there in the glass cases."

"Has anything ever truly scandalized you, Professor?"

They halted again.

"Why–yes," Madsen answered, "the 'Piltdown fraud.' Someone stole a jawbone and a few teeth relics and seeded them into the ground, claiming later that he found that particular site and discovered those pieces on the basis of his own brilliant intuition. *That*, Mr. Cole, was a real crime."

"What people do to each other is one thing–what they do to the facts is another, entirely?"

"I know how that sounds." Professor Madsen laughed good-naturedly. "Human beings start in murder and mayhem, proceed to greed and cheating, slip into rivalry and egotism, and end in downright prevarication and even inaccuracy." He laughed again, briefly. "Still, I know what I meant: we can't help what people do, can we, but we can do something about recovering the truth. For whatever that means." He put his hand to his forehead. "I think. Don't you agree?"

"Thanks." Cole smiled and held out his hand. "I just wanted your perspective."

Professor Madsen shook Cole's hand. "You didn't answer my question."

"I thought it was rhetorical. Bye."

* * *

Before he went home, Cole stopped back at the *Tribune*. Sally was still at the reception desk. She had a small package for him.

He unwrapped it right there, taking out a badge.

"From Sheriff Spahn," he said. "That's nice." He slipped it into a pocket. "Now I can arrest as well as fine you."

"I'm not holding anything back," Sally said. "I *gave* you the package. And here is a note from Mavis."

Fred Heinz came out of the newsroom, heading for home at the end of the day.

"Thanks," Cole said and read the note quickly, commenting on it to Heinz. "The Libby banks keep microfilm for ten years. They have Who's-again's checks. He always signed them 'V. Sypher.'"

Heinz had stopped. "So?" he asked.

"So why didn't he nickname himself Vee instead of Sy?"

"The Vee of eventual victory instead of the sigh of–whatever? Hey, maybe he did, to somebody. Listen, has anyone ever called you Willy?"

"My mother."

"What's your wife call you?"

"Will. And, all right, my best friend, Robert Sculli, calls me Wilbur. Fleming, the boss, calls me Cole. Other people call me Mister. Sally might start calling me Officer."

"See? A man's a different man and a different person, at different times, to different people. You, me, Sypher–all our secrets are alike. Where you headed?"

"Dropping by Unruh's before home."

They said good-bye to Sally and went outside. They stood on the sidewalk.

"Getting chilly. October. Season of the fall," Heinz said. "Listen, King Cole: are you going to fire him?"

"Not yet anyway. Take it easy."

"He's made a remark or two, behind your back, on your own style. That you don't have a style. 'Literary man!' I told him, 'that's the point in journalism, *not* to have style get in the way. Fair-haired Cole is the best at it.' I tell you, he has a jealous and devouring nature. Deeply suspect. I say guilty until proven innocent."

"Come on, that's not you talking."

Elaborately Fred Heinz looked all around behind him. "I seem to be the only one here. It must've been me."

Cole sucked in a cheek. "It's the desks almost touching one another in the newsroom. Too close quarters. Familiarity breeds contempt."

"Hey, you cliché-monger. He's just contemptible, that's all. I've been back there with Stoddard for three and a half years–and Forbis for six. No contempt there. Now, give us somebody like Mavis, and you can shorten the proverb."

"Familiarity–breeds! Why, you old–"

Fred Heinz was already moving off. He waved after him. "That's all– *just* old. 'Night!"

CHAPTER TWENTY-ONE

Ray Unruh lived in a triplex apartment. Cole pressed the bell button and said to himself, I will *not* slide my gumshoe through the doorway when he opens the door. Instead, when Unruh opened, Cole went right on by him into the living room.

"Then there's the direct approach," he said, "where you walk straight into a room." He saw a typewriter on the coffee table. He didn't bother reading the copy in it or beside it. He just pointed to it.

"Is that the chapter?"

"The what?"

"The chapter for your book, literary man."

"What are you talking about? And hello."

"You've known Joyce for a couple of days–and nights?–already."

"Yes."

"Why didn't you tell me? With a note, or in-between other assignments at the newsroom?"

"Oh, well. Sure, I'm writing it up," Unruh said, "that's all. I didn't want even to mention it until I finished it."

"Edited it, you mean." Cole's eyes moved over the room.

"Give me a break. I just wanted to hand in something well composed, that you'd appreciate, like Mavis's work."

"You brought her here?" Cole sat on the sofa.

"Not Mavis."

"Don't be funny."

"Joyce? Yeah. I figured she switched bars after the Sypher thing. I found it–and her."

Cole felt with the heel of each foot under the upholstered flounce of the sofa. He swooped down and brought up the tape recorder he found.

"You just pushed this under here when I rang."

"Naturally."

"So you *are* editing–taking out and putting in."

"I had it under the bed," Unruh motioned to his bedroom. "She didn't know. For Christ's sake. I'm editing out, all right–the private things. Don't listen."

Cole had his finger on the Rewind tab, ready to hear it. Unexpurgated, including preliminaries, the thing itself and, afterwards, for all Cole knew, maybe the claiming of a private trophy. A man had no rights over the intense or comic intimacy of others. He handed the machine to Unruh.

"Why did you hide it, though?"

"My mistake." Ray was fully himself now. "A new sign–'My mistake'–in blue letters on a field of yellow. Sorry. I really am."

"You're breaking my heart." Cole slid over to the far end of the sofa. "And holding back on me. Read what you have."

Unruh sat behind the typewriter. He gathered up his papers and read and interpolated from them. While Cole listened, Cole thought, first there is myself, then Ray Unruh, then Joyce Dayley, then the man known to her as Sy or Vee, and only *then* the true or real Virgil Sypher. How could all the fictions add up to the actual man? Still, Cole listened.

Sypher had been fired from Libby Dam. He then ran some dope. From Canada. Down and out, again. Close to the border. Approached, on his last dollar, in a Libby bar. Then, not wanting to do it anymore–or having served his limited, too familiar usefulness–he was paid off partly in Quaaludes or LSD, some of which he kept. He came back to Missoula, later, broke again, unemployed, on ignominious food stamps. Also fishing: earnestly, for food. Especially up the Blackfoot. Having noticed the Bonner mill, he decided finally to try for a job there. He told Joyce Dayley he would combine it with fishing that weekend. Another reason for returning to that exact Blackfoot spot, he told her, was that he had lost his fishing knife the day or so before and wanted to find it.

Unruh laid aside his papers and notes. "What dumb moron would bring a butcher knife instead?" he asked.

"Say that again."

"I said, what dumb–my God, Ambrose Johnson!"

Unruh found aspirin, somewhere immediately by him, and took one or two.

Cole asked, "Are they really aspirin?"

"Come on. Migraine's from frustration or excitement. Can I help it if I'm sensitive?"

Cole smiled. He stood up.

"Still, it's a drug, sort of. What are we so superior about?"

Who ever said–?"

"Nobody has to *say* anything," Cole said, heading for the door. "Never mind. And never mind the butler, I'll show myself out."

"Oh, the butler!" Ray Unruh said. "*He* did it."

At the door, Cole paused. "You didn't happen to ask Joyce Dayley how adequate Virgil Sypher was?"

Ray shook his head against the question. "Maybe you should've been here," he said, "not me."

Cole laughed. "And how was–"

"–she? Good."

"Then you won't mind seeing her again–and asking that about Sypher. Also, if she knows about Ambie Johnson."

"Sure."

"Only, let me know this time: on time, ahead of the chapter you're on."

Cole inclined his head briefly to the typewriter. Then he went out, closing the door behind him.

On the way home, he had to wait at a corner for a late Disposal Company truck to turn. It turned, and the sign on the side of it read: Your Independent G-Man–It May Be Garbage To You, But It's Our Bread and Butter. Cole stared at it. He drove home.

June had her skeptical look but had held supper. Later he raked some leaves and bagged them. After dark he looked at television with June, and then he read in bed and then he went to sleep.

Memorably.

Because, first, he had a long involved marvel of a dream, which he awoke at two-thirty in the morning to note down, right away, as Robert Sculli once suggested. And, second, because he had his little revelation toward morning.

CHAPTER TWENTY-TWO

After she felt her husband slip out of the bed, June Cole came out a little after and saw him bent over his typewriter in the den. Her look, finally, seemed filled with patient wonderment. He waved her back when he glimpsed her, an in-exasperate woman about to become exasperate, and continued to record and occasionally guess at and add on to his dream, for vivid recall and continuity. The back of his mouth still tasted like dry brass. He still felt some cold sweat.

I am outside a great cavernous place. Very quiet, dark. Suddenly a big blazing marquee sign comes on, "American Super Market," and it flashes off and another comes on, "PayLess," and blinks out and there is yet another flickering sign with something wrong about it, store personnel gathering to investigate it, "Family Chopping"–and I am inside; consulting a large wall map of the store, only it is a map of Missoula, with concentric circles on it.

I recoil, finding myself in front of the fish and meat department. I take a package of prawns. I feel something is wrong, and I see, through a clear plastic window of the package, that they are wooden chess pawns, not prawns. I protest to somebody in a white coat: "Not pawns, I say, I want–bones." This man, only a presence, leads me a little farther down the counter and disappears. On a placard I read, "Cold Shoulder/Of–" I cannot read "Of" what, though I try hard. I think I perceive a joke. I want to giggle but feel anxious, maybe frightened. I look up. In a shadowy recessed corner, well behind the meat display case, opposite me but darkened, is a concealed but huge man wielding a cleaver. I back away, saying curiously, "Don't worry," to the figure, backing off in agonized slow motion.

I meet Sheriff Spahn and try to speak to him but cannot get words out. I notice he has a regular holstered gun but also a banana half-exposed from each trouser pocket. He smiles, presents me a badge that turns into a nameplate, which he pins on me. It says, as I glimpse it, "Cole Slaw." I want to laugh outright but fear uncontrolled hysteria, and I suppress the urge and flee.

I find myself in another aisle, reaching for a box of cereal: "Crispy Critters," with a shadowy vehicular picture on the front; on the back are decals of an inappropriately smiling Frankenstein's monster and Dracula. I put it quickly down, but discover Fred Heinz looking at me. "You playing catch-up with me?" he asks, very satisfied. "That's right, I say, trying to be witty, but unable to think of anything. He touches my nameplate. "Cole Slaw," he says and then puts his finger to his lips. "City limits," he says and points behind me, as he leaves.

He has shown me the toy department. I pass dolls, limp or crooked or somehow awry, then a set of "Visible Man" and "Visible Woman" human anatomy educational toys. I pick one up and then I nervously drop it, it breaks resoundingly, and I flee.

I rush away, feeling like a criminal. At last I am at the checkout stands. Sally is chewing gum at a register: no, it is a switchboard. I wave and go on through. But I apparently have a basket, on the inside of which is a garbage bag of–I don't know what. The checkout helper is Ray Unruh. I tell him, "I have to get out of this dump." He wears a tape recorder strapped in front of him. "I'm taking inventory," he says, adding, "of everybody."

I ask him, "Where's the Chief?" realizing that I am shouting, "Who's the Chef?" A crowd of people is pressing about me. "You are," they say in chorus. "There's Mavis." Unruh points, and at the great plate glass front I go to Mavis who, like a delivery girl, hands me a folded Tribune *which I unfold and spread. A three-column headline reads, "Cole slain..." Through the enormous plate glass window I see a rose sunset. I am very calm. Upon a huge horizon the sun hovers beautifully, refuses to set.*

Cole finished. Most of what he had put down was true, but some of it was embellished. But, then again, what was true had already been embellished dream-work; and what was otherwise supplied was, in the theater of the mind, just as "true," wasn't it? Cole walked back to the bedroom.

He got into bed. June seemed restless. He kissed her on the neck.

"Ouch," she said. "You bit me."

"Oh. Sorry. But as long as you're awake," he said, upon her, "let's–"

* * *

Just before dawn, he startled himself awake, sitting bolt upright in bed.

June said, "What's the matter now?"

"Nothing. I know where Ambrose Johnson is."

"What?"

"Was, for sure. Is, maybe."

"Who's Ambrose Johnson?"

"I'd rather you didn't know."

"You wake me up at six o'clock in the morning to tell me you'd rather not tell me where a certain person is, or isn't?"

"Guilty!" he said, snuggling back down in bed. "Guilty, guilty."

CHAPTER TWENTY-THREE

Cole and Mavis and Ray were standing before the wall map in the *Tribune* newsroom.

"Where did we find that the knife came from?" Cole asked.

Heinz stopped typing. Stoddard was leaning forward. Forbis glided himself over in his roller desk chair.

"Flowers Hotel. Stolen somehow," Ray answered.

"Not necessarily. Probably the knife slipped into the garbage and was put out, with the rest, in the alley trash can."

"OK," Mavis said.

"We have one other piece of evidence–bits of evidence–plastic bits and pieces. Now, not long after the crime Sypher stopped at the PayLess gas station, where George Langley thought he noticed something bulking on the seat or floor over on the shadowed passenger's side."

"A plastic bag," Forbis said. "With at least some of the remains."

"That's right. A heavy-duty *disposal* bag. With Sypher headed to–" Cole looked at the wall map.

Mavis cried, "The garbage dump!"

"And that dog got his remains from there," Forbis concluded. "Came over and took it from under a heap in there."

"Or *was* there," Cole said, "on a regular or constant basis. Because he belonged there.

Was allowed anyway to patrol there, a recognized, privileged dog. Anyway, the outer circle of our map hits the dump exactly."

"So the knife found its way to central disposal at the dump where somebody recovered it," Mavis added.

"The green bits of plastic are from a trash bag," Ray said. "Circumstantial. But–!"

"The dog's range extends from the North Side to the dump, or vice versa. To which dump Sypher was going." Cole was definite. "Circumstantial but strong convergence."

Ray said, "Sypher worked at the dump!"

"No–Ambie Johnson did. It was *his* dog. We have to turn things around a little. Maybe Sypher was the dominant of the two, but Johnson had the steady job, at least after a while, at the dump. When Sypher came back to town, he stayed with Johnson, not the other way around."

"So is Ambrose there now?" Unruh had done all he could do to hold himself still.

"Calm down," Cole said. "All we have is a man working at and from a garbage dump who retrieves a butcher knife that comes out of a bag and supplies his knifeless cousin. Also trash bag or bags for gear or fish."

"What you said before–" Stoddard called over, "circumstantial."

"Right," Cole said. "Which is one reason why we proceed slowly. And there's another."

Unruh said, "He's big. Which figures at the crime site."

"Which makes him dangerous now, too, maybe," Forbis observed. "So everybody take it easy."

"And he's somewhat mentally disabled," Mavis said.

"I'm leaving," Forbis said, throwing his hands up and rolling back to his desk.

Mavis recalled something. "Do you remember what Sypher said a couple of times just after his arrest? About Dahl. He said, 'Garbage, garbage,' for a while."

"Meaning that sometimes a put-on," Cole observed, "as a friend of mine tells me, does put on, not off. Anyhow, we have a purpose: to match fingerprints, for the knife. Mavis, you go on looking for Johnson's address. Ray, for the moment, you still have a certain assignment with that gal you know. And I'll scout the dump, maybe catch sight of him, trace him home. Let's go." He added for Ray's benefit, "And work together."

* * *

Cole phoned the Missoula Disposal Company. He spoke to their bookkeeper-and-secretary.

"Does Ambrose Johnson work for you?"

"Why?"

"What do you mean, why? It's a simple question, ma'am. Who are you, may I ask? Well, Glenda, all I want to know is–Me? I'm Wilbur Cole."

98

"Wait a minute." Glenda talked, off-phone, to somebody else. Then she was back. "You from the paper?"

"Yes, as a matter of fact."

"Well, we don't discuss our staff like that. And Mr. Bensen said, why would you want to know?"

"So Johnson is still working for you?"

"Sorry, we're busy today."

"All I want is his address."

"I can't help you. Company policy."

"What's the problem?"

"Thank you." She hung up.

Cole sat there, collecting his thoughts. He guessed, it's Arnold Mutch all over again. They're probably paying big and stupid Ambrose Johnson below minimum wage. Sometimes Cole thought it was all *social* and economic, not psychological at all. He remembered that Bruce Dahl was a social worker, and–

That's when the City, State, and Western contingent decided to hold back the mid-morning news and try some of the pastries at a new bakeshop, and he joined them. They all left and went over to the place.

* * *

A good-looking girl took their order. She went to get coffee all around while the other three decided on substance.

Cole admonished Lyle Stoddard. "You said 'a hot cup of coffee,' right?"

"Right."

"So, strictly speaking, if she gives you a hot cup of cold coffee, you've got nothing to complain about."

Forbis clapped Stoddard on the back. "See? Never take the Assistant Editor out on your break."

Unruh came in, saw them, came over. He held up his arm in stiff awkward greeting–Cole had the swift terripilated impression of a Nazi salute–but Unruh said, "How!"

Lyle Stoddard said, "*Our* Indians don't say How…they say when–"

Before he could finish it, Heinz and Forbis did it for him: "–they already *know* how."

The girl brought their coffees. She stood prettily, took pastry orders, and left.

Unruh said, "I'd like to ask *her* when."

Nobody said anything.

Fred Heinz said, "She's a really nice girl."

"I haven't any prejudice of race, color, creed," Unruh said, "or niceness. I'm just broad-minded."

Heinz either dropped or flung down his coffee spoon.

Unruh looked across the table to him, smiling slowly. "Oh," he pointed his question, "no hard feelings–anymore?"

Heinz, livid and lunging somewhat over the table, missed Ray Unruh, who had slid his chair back in time. Stoddard and Forbis, on each side of Heinz, pulled him back down. Unruh took out a half-dollar, stood up and put it deliberately by his cup and saucer.

"Back in the office," Heinz said in a level voice, "don't talk to me again–ever."

"Very witty, bustard," Ray said. He included all in his parting remark to Cole. "Everybody hear that right? He's a rare bird–that's all I could possible mean in this august company. Or is it October, with Halloween coming?"

He went out.

Cole said, while the other three looked at him, "Two weeks to go. He's on the payroll till the end of the month. That'll be all."

"Too long," Fred Heinz said.

"Getting worser and worser," Stoddard said. "There's bad grammar for you."

"That's not all that's unprintable," Forbis said.

"When he first said what he said," Cole confessed, "I didn't get it for a moment."

Heinz reached over and patted Cole's arm companionably. "I believe it. That's just you."

Afterwards, they had their orders, paid and left. The other three went back to the *Tribune*. They seemed perfectly all right.

Cole went over to the sheriff's office.

CHAPTER TWENTY-FOUR

"I just can't barge into something or start assigning a full-time officer to a fugitive who isn't a fugitive," Max Spahn said, "on a case that isn't a case anymore. I can't even keep up with the bona fide APBs that we get, plus normal complaints."

"Suppose we locate Ambrose Johnson on our own?"

"And find exactly what?"

"That prints match. Would you bring him in for questioning then?"

"Maybe."

"That's good enough for me."

"That's not what counts," Sheriff Spahn said. "Will it be good enough for the County Attorney now?"

* * *

At lunch in the mall, Sculli said, "I read your dream."

"Was it too–composed?" Cole asked.

"Yes. But the clever parts are so close to the unconscious, it's useful anyway."

"Oh?" Cole arched his eyebrows.

"I'm not going to mention what you expect me to–the monster backs of the cereal boxes, or the dolls that break, and so on. But there's another detail that's especially interesting."

"What?"

"The figure lurking behind the counter."

"Ambie Johnson."

"You backed away from him, but you told *him* not to worry. Fascinating."

"Isn't that simple reversal or displacement?"

Robert Sculli shook his head. "You're up on terminology, but–no. Do you appreciate the fact that for some time now you are guessing that Ambrose Johnson–whom you call 'Ambie,' how's that for ambiguous?–is the technical criminal, not Virgil Sypher?"

"I suppose so. He thought he was protecting Virgil, for a change. Effected maybe by those TV monster movies, and under drug influence too, he maybe enlarged some argument in his own mind between Dahl and Sypher–and did what he did. Then Virgil arranged the rest, and fled, and got himself arrested, knowing Ambrose later could not quite be trusted to remember–anything."

"It's also interesting that you are calling them by their first names more and more."

"Because of the confusing personal affections grimly involved?"

"That's your question, you answer it. The final dream witticism, by the way, of 'Cole slain'–"

104

"That's my secret suicidalism?"

Sculli tugged at his earlobe. "Well, more like your innocence slain."

"At this late date?"

"Of course. There are people who can't absorb the Holocaust. And other things. They know, they know, all right, but they can't *believe* yet. Each of us comes to certain recognitions in his own lifetime, if ever. Never mind abstract theory just now. The thing is, I'm getting a trifle nervous about hulking Ambrose Johnson, as the tempo of things increases."

"As a matter of fact, I'll be doing something in that regard this afternoon."

"Be careful."

"Oh yes. I'm *not* suicidal."

"Well, just don't be too damn pleased with yourself that things are moving so well. Events get beyond us. Don't lose anything more than your sweet innocence."

CHAPTER TWENTY-FIVE

Cole drove into the garbage dump, at about 4:30 P.M. There was a tiny cubicle office for the watchman or foreman. He was in there with his door open when Cole pulled up and stopped a little distance away.

Before Cole got out of the car he took off his tie and jacket and quickly rolled up his sleeves two turns. Then he got out and sauntered over to the cubicle. The man inside wore a checked shirt open at the neck with his sleeves all the way up, though it was chilly in the October sun.

Cole waved and smiled and asked casually, "Does Ambie Johnson still work here?"

The man stood up. He nodded but said, "He's not here, though."

"Coming in on a truck?"

"Nope."

Cole waited. The man did not explain.

"Wilbur Cole." Cole shook the man's hand.

"Benjy Phillips." He was a wizened old man, with a pleasant toothless grin. His eyes were narrowed, though.

"He's working," Cole tried, "but not working today?"

"That's right. He's on vacation, sort of."

"I just wanted to get ahold of him. You know where he lives?" Phillips shook his head. "Well, somebody on one of the trucks must know."

Philips started shaking his head again and then stopped, looking at Cole directly. "You the police?"

Cole took out his wallet. He did not say anything. After showing the badge, he put back his wallet. Mr. Phillips scratched his head. He glanced behind him at a walkie-talkie. Cole edged around Phillips and put his hand on it and stared profoundly at the old man.

"You see, he's moving just now." Mr. Phillips explained that one of their drivers, Mark Sperry, was genuinely taking his vacation now, coinciding with a steelhead run in Idaho. Before Sperry took off, he helped Johnson move to a new place. "Johnson ain't quite right," Mr. Phillips whirred his index finger around his temple. "He don't rightly know what a vacation *is* exactly, he thinks the driver and him quit for a time."

Cole felt softly stunned by mere involvements. "Events," he said under his breath.

"Hey?"

"Anybody around who knows his old address?"

Mr. Phillips hunched his shoulders.

Cole studied him. The old man's forehead was crinkled and his eyes were still narrowed, now against the setting sun. But it would be his only deception. Cole decided he was looking at an open placid face. The dissimulator here was not Phillips but Wilbur Cole.

"Bye," he said. "Thanks."

Mr. Phillips nodded, half-smiled.

Cole got into his car and started it up. Then he leaned out of the window and spoke to Mr. Phillips, who was standing there in his little doorway.

"Do the end men on the trucks still have sticks or crowbars tucked in back somewhere, against big dogs?" And good for fingerprints.

"Yep." Mr. Phillips said. "But not Johnson."

"No?"

Mr. Phillips grinned, raising his arms to indicate a big, a huge man. "He don't need no club."

Phillips brought down his arms and now spread the fingers of both his hands in a graphic throttling manner. He–and Cole–watched his hands, imagined them as gigantic. "He strangles them up, with his bare hands." Their eyes met now. "I recollect, he got holt of a police dog once," Phillips said, "on the South Side last month–and flinged him into some bushes–unconscious."

Mr. Phillips laughed soundlessly now. Cole waved, backed his car, turned around and left. He was smiling, himself. That was because he admired and had not expected Mr. Phillips' probably quick-minded rewrite of the dog breed. At the same time, he felt little horripilations across the back of his scalp.

* * *

Next morning, heading for his newsroom desk, Cole waved at the wall map.

108

"We don't need that anymore," he said. "Ambrose Johnson works at the dump."

He sat at his desk. Ray Unruh came over.

"I just wanted to say, I have re-Joyced."

It took Cole a moment. "Oh. You're really reporting on Virgil?"

"He experienced a lot of *sexualis promptitudinous*. Funny, though, I have the feeling by now that she not only liked him anyway, but preferred him."

"Maybe that's because your Kraft is Ebbing," Cole said, "all the way around."

Unruh made a face and went back to his desk. Now Mavis came over.

"I finished that other ecology piece." She put some papers on his desk. "And I tried at the State Equalization Office–on Ambrose Johnson's withholding statements–but they wouldn't give me any information."

"They don't give him any paid vacation at the Dump, I figure. But they certainly must pay him for work. Wait a minute, let me try something."

He rang up the Helena number Mavis gave him.

"Hello. This is Deputy Cole in Missoula. With Sheriff Spahn. Yes. Can you please furnish the last address filed for an Ambrose Johnson? Sure. I'll wait." He said to Mavis, "They have it, they'll give it."

And they did.

"Get Ray," he said. "I want you both–two at a time–to visit the place."

"For safety?"

"No, he's not there–he just moved. But maybe one of you can talk and distract the landlord, say, while the other–with gloves or handkerchief–heists an unwashed spoon or something out of there. Oh Lord," he caught himself. "What are we exactly, the cops–or the robbers?"

CHAPTER TWENTY-SIX

Mavis and Unruh succeeded in contacting the landlord and meeting him in order to look at the repainted shack. Mavis explained to Cole about how they went in there posing as husband and wife (if she shuddered, was it the proximity to Ambrose Johnson–or Ray Unruh?) and were shown around. The landlord was puzzled, since they were not the type of clients he would have expected–and maybe also because Mavis kept nervously and gaily opening and closing kitchen and other cabinet drawers and Unruh kept lagging in some other room and even had "to go" to the bathroom once. Peculiar and thorough as they were, however, they found nothing–not a leftover spoon or crow bar or old garbage can or anything. The bright little house was completely empty and redone.

That was all. Except that, at the end, the piqued landlord finally asked them to leave. "You're not even married. You ought to be ashamed," he said. Mavis glanced at Ray Unruh and said, "I *am* sorry," to the landlord, who was somewhat mollified. But then, at the door, Ray flicked the light switch on and off rapidly so that the overhead light flashed like a photographer's bulb. "Smile!" he said, "Thank you!" He was getting his kicks out of it, Mavis said, though he still carried his little jar of aspirin and took two in the car on the way back.

* * *

Cole spoke to Ray and Mavis.

"So that didn't work either. We've got a week before he returns to the job, and then we'll figure something out. Meanwhile, one more assignment each. Ray, go back and find out anything at all on *Tim Sypher*, in or around Butte. Mavis, go to the Deer Lodge prison and find out from the warden, or anyone else there, about Sypher's death." He sat back.

Mavis hesitated. "And–you?"

"Oh, I'm just going to sit and think."

"You're leaving the dangerous part for us, eh?" Ray said.

"No," Cole answered, lacing his hands behind his head. "I'm leaving the dangerous part for *me*."

* * *

Some nights later, Cole sat in his den, going back over reports he'd had Ray and Mavis write out for him. He was skimming Unruh's:

"Except for two humdrum matters, Tim Sypher is clean. And in Butte, the exceptions hardly count, like parking tickets. Once, he got hauled in on a big Saturday night brawl, with some other lodge types–I think, V.F.W.–but they were all let go later. Another time he was caught for hunting out of season and without a license, which he must have done other times, only this time he was caught and fined. He's just a hard drinking eager-maniac–"

Cole sighed and put down Unruh's report. He reached over for Mavis' findings and re-read them also.

"In his ninth month of incarceration Virgil Sypher jumped or was pushed over the rail of the walk along the third tier of cells in Block C at the Deer Lodge State Penitentiary. It certainly could have been murder, the warden thought. Inmates have their unwritten law against certain kinds of criminals, like rapists, kidnappers–and cannibals, too. He said no one saw him leap, either those on the tier or guards below. And nobody *heard* anything until it was over. There had been no cry. The prison psychiatrist believed it was suicide. Self-execution. Guilt. Or the homosexual confinement. Or just the confinement, you might say. What strikes *me* is it was the ninth month he was there. He was delivered."

Cole slowly tapped Mavis' report on the top of his desk. Then he let it go. He walked around the room a couple of times. "Delivered from– what?" he asked himself. He stopped pacing finally. He wanted to formulate his thinking now.

I'll tell it to Sculli, he thought.

CHAPTER TWENTY-SEVEN

"So Virgil left the Bonner mill and started walking up along the Blackfoot, that Saturday. Ambrose Johnson was either up there from the day before or would come later for the weekend."

Wilbur Cole paced Robert Sculli's living room. Sculli had moved the coffee table and then the footstool of his easy chair from their middle room positions.

"I think he was up there already," Cole said, "with his sleeping bag (which, if he still has it, we could check for possible blood stains), maybe a rod, and that moronically salvaged knife, belted or stuffed in with the rest in the salvaged green plastic trash bags. There they are for the balance of the day. Bruce Dahl comes in that evening."

"Fate," Sculli remarked. "Dahl was almost an accessory, stumbling into a psycho-drama he had nothing to do with."

"Coincidence or doom, what's the terrifying difference?"

"All right–go on."

"There are alternate scenarios. An argument–political or religious–and Dahl trying to kill Sypher."

"Dahl–?"

"Because *he* had the gun. I'll get to that. The point is, they got to talking with and knowing each other for a couple of hours. Yes, Ambrose and Virgil are a little under Quaaludes or something, but there's enough consciousness in Virgil to get the essence of Dahl and all the contrasts: Virgil's almost hysteric joblessness/Dahl's on-the-job off-the-road holiday; hitchhiking/that beautiful foreign car; Sypher's fishing out of at least partial need/and the slightly dandified sportsman. The initially

114

hearty, companionable Dahl slowly but surely revealing himself as the big cynic and hypocrite. The flag-carrying school kid with grown-up social service spoils–BMW, bamboo fly rod, mummy sleeping bag. Grim joke. He even snuggles into it for the night. You see, he's 'got to get up early' for those fish–like a task. Anyway, *he* can't spend all day; he envies *them*. Or maybe, at some point, he scorns Virgil as a gross and illegal bait fisherman. Something like that. We'll never know the ignition point. All we know is that, at last, Virgil explodes."

"But he doesn't kill him?"

"Not at first. He's enraged and jealous, but he doesn't stab him, if that's what you mean. Yes, he had the knife, but Dahl was shot before he was–well the pathologist's report says he was shot first."

"As to that, how would Sypher know there was a gun in Dahl's glove compartment?"

"He wouldn't know and didn't get it. So it has to be that Dahl, frightened or angered himself, scrambles back out of his sleeping bag, runs to the car, gets the gun–"

Sculli registered an audible sigh. "The agent of society. That appeals to you. You want *him* guilty of *some*thing."

"He *is*. There are no other explanations possible."

"There are, any number."

"They'd be too strained. The easier the truer. Dahl came out with gun drawn or waving it, or–in fact–shooting at Virgil. The trees may have bullets buried in them. Anyway, they wrestled and–"

"–Sypher got the gun away from him and–maybe even by accident– shot him?" Sculli asked.

"Accidentally on purpose, or purposely accidental–or even in self-defense: he shot and killed this model of complacent, self-contained security and success, toward whom he may even have yearned somewhat, also envied, also hated."

"And the car is like an admired body. From whose recesses came the phallic gun."

"I leave that part to you. But after violent action, with LSD or whatever still in him, Virgil zonks out. And that brings us to Ambrose: Ambrose."

"Ah."

"When Virgil finally comes to, a good deal later in the night–Dahl is not only dead but dismembered."

"Because one of the two–it had to be Sypher–threw up."

"Exactly. Ambrose was more psychologically as well as physically capable of the old forest butchery: in a trance himself then, in fantasied woods again with Uncle Tim Sypher and company–lightning, northern lights, firelight–afraid at first, satisfied at the kill later; also himself the clean-up boy–for deer, elk, antelope, bear–poached game to be stowed out of sight in bags, which Ambrose just happened to have by him!"

"So there was no cannibalism, strictly speaking. Only a hypnoidal re-enactment of animal dismemberment? And the knife forgotten in some tree in the dark, after the blubbery heart was virtually taken out."

"That's right," Cole said.

"Oh? Well, let's get to the end of it, in your mind."

Cole paced again. "After Virgil's own retching and revulsion and the panicked hauling of the torso into the river, the other remains and the gun, too, are kept in the bag or bags Ambrose had put them in."
116

"Go on."

"Ambrose was probably blanked out himself by then, and taken home, undressed, his clothes disposed of with the rest, the heaped bag or bags glimpsed in shadow by the Payless gas attendant. Then Virgil goes to the dump, leaving Ambrose behind to revive and dimwittedly forget that he ever had anything to remember."

"Meanwhile, the symbolism is suggestive," Sculli remarked. "The trashing is revenge and punishment. And the later idea of 'I am a cannibal' is an added fantasy or wish, partly true, after all. Together with the subsequent flight and arrest–and self-conviction. To safeguard Ambrose, yes, but also to pay for his own complicity."

Cole started from his seat.

"But the fingers!"

Sculli said, "Not crucial. Cannily, he provisioned himself for the arrest."

"That seems to make it too extra-calculating."

"Well the major difference between us is that I take a psychological approach, mostly, and you a moral one, mostly. Some things fall outside your view."

Cole looked at Robert Sculli. "Am I wrong?" He stood up, finished, about to leave. "No," he answered himself, "I'm not. I'm not."

CHAPTER TWENTY-EIGHT

On Monday morning Cole took two calls in the newsroom. Marge Sculli was suddenly taken to the hospital; she would undergo surgery for an abdominal cyst as large as an orange.

And the sheriff phoned. "Max Spahn here. Listen–the current County Attorney won't hear of anything."

"You mentioned prospective fingerprints?"

"He doesn't care. 'You want us to send out delayed pix and flyers, to shake up some logger's two-year-old memory, too?' That's what he says. Sorry, Wilbur, I just can't go out and bring somebody in. But–"

"What?"

"If there's a ruckus–any place, about anybody, over anything–that's something else again. Once we have a man in on one thing, we can go ahead on another. You hear?"

"Yes." Cole thought a moment. "Max, can you have a car ready at, say, about 5:15 tomorrow? For the North Side probably?"

Spahn said, "No. That's city jurisdiction, anyhow. Tell you what, I'll be fifteen minutes late going home tomorrow, because I'll just happen to be visiting the Chief of Police's office. Call in there for me if you need to; I'll ride with a cop. But one way or the other–"

"I know, be careful."

"No, I wasn't going to say that. You know, sometimes you're wrong. I was going to say something else."

"What?"

"Be *extra* careful."

"Oh. Nothing will happen. These are just precautions. What we call routine, right? Thanks. And bye."

"So long," Spahn said.

* * *

Cole hung up. Then he motioned over Mavis and Unruh.

"Anything on Johnson?" they asked.

"Mark Sperry, the dump truck driver, and he will be back tomorrow. So finish the Obits and Society page," Cole said to Unruh, and to Mavis, "Wind up the cougar rewrite. Tomorrow I'll go to the dump, Mavis will be on the street, and we'll communicate through Ray here at the *Tribune*."

"Me?" Ray Unruh said.

"Yes."

"Women's lib," Mavis said with a triumphant quaver in her voice. "But I'm a little scared."

"Nothing's going to substantially happen. You'll locate a phone or phone booth, and so will I, and we can just call in."

"We ought to have CBs or something," Ray said.

"Don't get gadgety," Cole responded. "We don't have to mechanize ourselves or dramatize anything. Either I simply get the address from the driver or someone, or I trail Johnson back, or Mavis spots the truck that picks him up or drops him off, and we let one another know. Nobody acts alone, that's all."

"Because," Unruh said, "the life you save may be your own."

Cole looked at him piteously. "Can't we get you that job in Pocatello–or Brisbane? You're our liaison man–not witty commentator."

Unruh said, "And, coincidentally on purpose, out of the action."

"*What* action? Phoning in? When the time comes, we'll all go over there, together."

Heinz turned from his typewriter and asked, "And do what, by the way?"

"I don't know yet. Confuse him, make some sort of low-level ruckus."

Heinz clapped his hands softly and called over to Stoddard and Forbis, "In the new Judo-Christian tradition."

Cole said, "Go away–all of you." He swooped up his topcoat, however. "No, *I'm* the one who's going," he said, heading for the hospital.

CHAPTER TWENTY-NINE

Only Mr. Phillips was at the dump the next morning. All trucks were out. Mark Sperry's was doing the North Side that morning, Mr. Phillips reported, so he had simply gone over that way and picked up Ambie Johnson at his new place.

Cole left, intending to come back and check again a little before noon. Mavis had called in twice to the *Tribune*, having missed seeing the truck. She decided to stop patrolling the streets and would now park someplace central, taking an hour or so's chances on the law of averages.

"George Averages," Unruh said. "Governor from 1930 to 1934— signed a law about garbage trucks having to return to the scene of the grime."

Cole said, "Will you just finish the Society Page and take Mavis' calls?"

Ray was jaunty or, rather, nervous-jaunty. "Actually I was just writing up 'the return of Mr. Mark Sperry from steelhead fishing on the exclusive banks of the Clearwater. Mr. Sperry is premier chauffeur of Missoula's Civic Sanitary Engineering and'–"

Cole's phone rang. It was Robert Sculli's receptionist to say that Mrs. Sculli had taken a turn for the worse in post-operative care.

At 11:30 Cole drove back to the Missoula Disposal dump. Maybe they had or would come back for a lunch break. At noon Mr. Phillips looked at his watch.

"Won't come," he said.

At the northwest end of the dump, by the little cubicle office, there was almost no odor. It was cloudless and sunny today, though a sharp coolness cut through the air. Cole was out of his car, standing, looking up the valley. He had one of those unexpected moments of unbidden beauty again. It was all the more surprising since he was looking at nothing in particular–mountain range, or peak, or sloped hillside, or valley– contemplating nothing individuated in the view. But all at once there was a lull of traffic on the nearby interstate and, in the hush and the crisp brittle air in this least likely corner, the whole landscape suddenly blurred for him in a melted lambent haze of gold light. That was all. Mr. Phillips was asking him something. The cars came thrumming back. Cole blinked his eyes, as if squeezing them against the sunshine. Then he consciously looked at and listened to the old man.

"What did you say you wanted him for?" Mr. Phillips repeated.

"Johnson? I want to talk with him."

"Can't. He's dumb."

Cole just stood there. Mr. Phillips was pointing to his own mouth.

"You mean Ambrose Johnson can't talk?" Cole said.

"Can't hardly. Can't hear too well either. Claims it was from mostly a 'lectrical accident." The old man grinned his open candor once more. "So nobody knows for sure what's inside," he pointed to his temple. "Could be dumb both ways. Then again–"

Cole went to his car door, about to leave. He glanced at the walkie-talkie in the tiny cabin.

"So you all look after him? Maybe *you* even called Sperry today on the truck, though that won't keep the rest of us away forever. How much do you know, Mr. Phillips?"

"Generally?" he chuckled. "Or about Johnson? I been here now five and a half years, more than everybody else except Johnson. They pass

122

him, sort of, from one to another, to take care of a little—though he's still a big, strong feller. All I know is, what with one thing and another, a man can't shake hands with hisself."

After a moment Cole said, "I respect your loyalty." He looked all about him there. "Thank you. I've got to go," he said.

* * *

Mavis called in to Unruh to say she had not spied the truck over lunch hour either. Sally had another message, about Marge Sculli, for Cole—something was wrong—and he drove to the Community Hospital.

Marge Sculli was hemorrhaging. In his powerlessness and travail Robert Sculli looked stern, even angry. They sat together. Once Wilbur put his hand on Sculli's shoulder. Sculli just sat, rock-like. At about 2:30 a doctor came by to report some stabilization.

Sculli roused himself, found out that Cole'd had no more lunch than he, and took him to the staff cafeteria. When they came back to Marge's floor, Cole broke away temporarily to get Unruh on the phone. Ray was ebullient.

"Mavis called in. She spotted a company truck. *The* truck, probably. Parked across the street from that old NP bar! He's having one with the boys."

Cole looked at his watch. It was 4:10.

"A little premature."

"Probably take up twenty minutes," Unruh figured. "Then they'll drop him off and cruise back in to the dump yards at about 5. Very mature, actually."

"I don't know if I'll be anywhere but here," Cole said.

"Oh? Listen, let me–"

"Just wait for Mavis' call. Stay put. I'll get back to you."

* * *

Things eased at the hospital. And June Cole came in.

It was now 4:40. Cole rang up the *Tribune* again. Unruh reported that Mavis had not called back. Cole decided to wait at the floor phone booth, clearing Ray's line and staying right there for his return call this time.

When the booth phone rang, although he was expecting it, Cole felt jarred, all through him.

"It's me," Ray Unruh said. "They dropped him off, all right–a great big sonofabitch, Mavis said–"

"No, she didn't. You did."

"Have it my way–a great big sonofabitch, and she trailed 'em–and we've got the address."

124

"All right, take it easy." Cole was trying to think. He looked up the hall, where June stood outside the door of Marge Sculli's room, where Robert had gone in. "I don't think I'll be leaving here right away."

"Let me and Mavis–"

"Wait. Wait." Cole was gauging time.

Ray Unruh said, "I meant he's a great big easygoing sonofabitch, probably. We've been talking ourselves into a lot of things, including how much of a big dumb dangerous ox he is and now you find out it's really deaf-and-dumb, and it'll turn out that he's next to harmless. Anyway I can protect myself and take care of anything. But there won't be anything."

"Maybe. But it happens he's just been drinking."

"It was only twenty minutes. One draft beer. Lots of foam in that bar. Not serious drinking. *I'm* getting to be an expert. *I*–"

"Hold it up," Cole said.

"OK!" Unruh said. He must have let go or slammed the receiver.

* * *

Robert came out of Marge Sculli's room a relieved man, almost happy. No visitors were allowed just yet, but she was better than stabilized, she was all right. June Cole was going to stay with Robert. They urged Wilbur to go.

Cole went back to the booth phone.

Unruh did not answer his call.

Cole redialed to Sally. Unruh was gone.

"Where?" Cole asked.

"To Mavis, I guess."

"I know *that*. But specifically–" There was no sense in blowing up at Sally, and he ought not shout anyway (though he wanted to put aside the phone and scream across town). "Look on my desk, will you, and see if he left a memo."

She did.

"Nothing doing," she came back to tell him.

"God almighty," Wilbur Cole said.

"Wait a sec," Sally said. She was away for a minute. The pulse beat in Cole's temples.

"It's 402 Calder Street," Sally said. "I *think*," she added maddeningly. "Let me put it on a lamp again."

"What?"

She came back, repeating the address. "That street is on the North Side, isn't it?"

"Yes!"

126

She had gotten Ray Unruh's hand-written–and hard written–
impression on the pad page beneath the address he had noted down from
Mavis. Sally had torn off that second not altogether blank page and held
it against a lamp bulb, and deciphered it.

"Sally," Cole said: "you're a honey. Can you call the City Police but
ask for Sheriff Spahn and tell him to meet me at that address? Quick."

He said goodbye to Robert and June. And he went doubling down the
hospital stairs and outside into his car. He knew Unruh would claim,
passing it on to Mavis, that he'd understood Cole to say, "Hold him up."
Something like that.

The thing was, could Cole get there in time? Before what, exactly?
He did not, could not know. His premonition would not form itself. But it
hovered almost visibly in the time and distance now directly ahead of
him, and a piercing sound rose to a crescendo somewhere until he
realized it was inside his own head.

CHAPTER THIRTY

Cole got there late, of course, and only with what Mavis told him could he reconstruct what happened. As a slight drizzle started, Ray Unruh had driven up and parked behind her car in front of Ambrose Johnson's dilapidated set-back bungalow, joining her for a conference, after Cole's alleged go-ahead. They would pose as renters again, mistaking the house, braving out Ambie Johnson's ineffectual protest as they quick-talked themselves through a tour of the rooms, opened a drawer in the kitchen or inspected a bathroom on one side of the house and simultaneously a closet on the other, one of them at least hoping to find tableware or a clothes hanger or something else portable. Mavis wanted to wait for Cole, but Ray said Cole wasn't coming and went ahead and knocked on the door.

Johnson opened the door. Ray asked to come in. Johnson (warned by Mr. Phillips, Mark Sperry?) uncomprehendingly, hugely, blocked the passage, waving or pressing them off.

Unruh found his inspiration. "Don't push!"

Quickly, Mavis went down the cracked and buckling flag path, onto the sidewalk. Then she turned. She saw Ambrose Johnson on his rough hewn stone porch, Unruh below him and back a few steps and then she saw but did not understand the first of three or four popped flashes in the gloaming, Unruh using the instamatic camera from one of his pockets to photograph–and startle–and electrify–the big man looming above and before him. Unruh said something too, but Mavis could not hear the goad, already wisely stepping over the curb, into the gutter, on and around to the other side of the car away from the sidewalk, turning again to look at Johnson, now descending the flag path after Unruh, herself trying to decide now whether to get in her car or Unruh's or run for it, hearing Ray Unruh say something like, "Here, you can–have–hold–the

128

camera," and then the sound of it flung and shattered, Mavis getting into her car, now behind her wheel, frantically locking all doors, nobody visible anymore on the flag path or sidewalk but a tumultuous struggle going on nearby–from the grass sward between sidewalk and curb (and inside the car: Mavis trying insanely to find her keys: amoeboid headlights now coming down the street behind, squirming in her mirror, also in her mind's eye as other lights had exploded below the rough stone porch, all lights jumbled in the onrushing dark). And then she heard a shot, not believing it, thinking that the firing of the gun drawn from Unruh's pocket was a tire blow-out on her own unmoving and even unstarted car, disbelieving and disoriented as she was steeped in her plasmal fear. She got hold of and then lost her keys (slipped from sweat moistened hands to the floorboard), while the headlights of Cole's car drew up behind Unruh's and she suddenly now believed in a series of real bullets and, though she never truly passed out, she felt heard and saw nothing but the strict black light of her own shimmering consciousness in some middle distance.

The shots Cole heard *he* knew were real shots, not because he wasn't experiencing the seethe of sensation Mavis underwent but because he guessed, at once and too late, that they came from Ray Unruh's revolver "protection", bought after his first Butte interview and then his experience with Bitterroot rancher Arnold Mutch and then his North Side visits in general. Already Unruh was rolling up, and Johnson lay on the margin of damp grass near the sidewalk, there by Cole's stopped feet. "He came after me!" Unruh protested. Cole said, "Shut up!" thrusting Unruh back, and kneeling down. Just before the whirl of flashing lights and the audible siren of the police car came furiously down the street, Cole bent to Johnson, who seemed to be trying to say something, something plaintive before his head lolled over. It was almost completely dark now but Cole made out Johnson's slack body on the grass, long legs and outsized feet extending over the curb, and he stood back up.

"You just killed Ambrose Johnson. Now you've got, not your by-line, but a big magazine special, right? Or that million dollar book. You deliberately misheard me on the phone and then baited him. You—*you're* the real cannibal."

"Well, I'm not alone. It's dog-eat-dog, remember?" He pointed to Johnson. "He was only a retard, what are you so riled up about?"

"You absolute—"

"Not absolute," Unruh said, "everything's relative. You put me on it, remember. And this'll get me straight to the coast from here—"

Spahn's voice broke in: "You'll have to get out of jail first." They put handcuffs on Ray Unruh. Cole heard them snap on through the drizzle. Spahn said, "Routine, huh?" passing Cole on their way to the police car.

Over his shoulder Ray called back, "Check the camera pieces for fingerprints. I was the best reporter you actually had."

"Go on," Cole said, "get out of here."

"It's a pleasure," Unruh said before they put him in the police car.

The siren had whined terrifically down, but the lights of it were still rotating in mostly crimson revolutions.

CHAPTER THIRTY-ONE

"So," Sculli asked, "Ray Unruh's in jail?"

Cole laughed hollowly. "No. He's out on his own 'recognizance,' and if they go ahead with a trial, he'll get acquitted for self-defense. Maybe they'll commend him for civic-mindedness."

"I don't think so," Sculli said.

Cole thought for a moment. "And me—did I in some way arrange for Ambrose Johnson's execution?"

"Possibly. It's interesting, though, that for all of the Sypher principle in you, you showed up finally as Society."

"My own split personality again?"

"Ah," Sculli either said or breathed.

"What really bothers me, though, is that I was prepared to lose a story—but not a life."

They were standing in Sculli's back yard under a tree.

"Funny word you newspaper people use—'story.'"

"Yet we're after the truth."

Sculli patted Cole's shoulder, wordlessly.

"Still," Cole went on, "'story' is an apt word. Especially for all the ironies it can cover."

"Like Ambrose Johnson's peril, from Unruh, and not the other way around?"

"Yes. And bubble-gum Sally turning brilliant in a crisis. Beats me."

Sculli put his arm around Cole. "About reversals: when you came to the hospital, you not only dropped your work for me, you were, for a little while there, exchanging paternalism with me. And there's one more instance." He took down his arm and pointed toward his house, from which they could hear the two women laughing about something.

"What?" Cole asked.

"Marge's operation. I don't mean only that the cyst was benign. Picture the surgeon masked, gloved, knife-wielding, but for beneficent mutilation. Think about that. And Marge gratefully under anesthetic *drugs*."

"Yes."

They headed for the house.

"Let's join the ladies," Sculli said, and they did.

* * *

Quite late after lunch, Mavis phoned in to the *Tribune*. Cole took it at his newsroom desk in the back. The thing was, she had just gotten engaged–to Ollie Blastic, Professor Zachary Wyld's assistant in wildlife management. Cole told her to take the rest of the day off. "And congratulations, Mavis!" He hung up.

Heinz said, "So she landed *some*body? Excuse me for eafdropping."

"Yes. Eaf?" Cole knew better than to look from Fred Heinz to Lyle Stoddard, but he did.

Stoddard thought a moment. "Plural–eaves, singular eaf. He supposedly overheard just this one thing."

Cole just accepted that, nodding.

But Forbis joined in. "Wait a second. Then it was: Adam and Eaf?"

"No," Heinz said. "It was Eve–she was one too many for him."

Cole reached over to his VRT, fingering the keys. "I can't hyphenate or *justify* any of this," he said.

There was a pause.

"I think," Forbis said, "that that qualifies him. All those in favor of permanently hiring him as a fair-haired boss say so."

Stoddard said, "Aye."

Fred Heinz fetched out a five-by-seven framed photograph from his drawer and brought it over to Cole. It was an enlarged picture of himself. The thing was, they had gotten Carl Atkins to touch it up with an Indian headdress on Cole, quite well done.

Heinz said, "Here you are, Chief." He set it gently on Cole's desk.

"And," he said: "How!"

Cole sat back in his chair. He found that his hands were under each pressing thigh. To keep them from his eyes, probably–which were slowly, damnably brimming.

* * *

He dropped in on Max Spahn and gave him back his badge.

"You don't want to know what we might have found at Johnson's?" Spahn asked.

"No. Case closed–closed closed."

They walked to the door together.

"The prints?" Spahn suggested.

"Don't tell me."

Spahn laughed. "We're reversing positions." He pointed back to the badge lying on his desk. "You sure you don't want to hang on to it, just like that?"

"I'm through with it."

"You can have it as a gift."

They shook hands.

"I prefer the good will," Cole said. "Bye."

"So long," Spahn said, grinning.

CHAPTER THIRTY-TWO

Cole had lunch downtown with Mavis and Ollie. Afterwards, passing an Arts and Crafts shop, on impulse he ushered them inside, to buy Mavis an engagement present. She chose a filigreed, delicate copper bracelet. He paid for it at the counter. Mavis looked up at the wall.

"Oh look," she said, pointing to a ferocious necklace, made of bear claws, hanging on the wall behind the register.

"What about it?" Cole asked.

"There was one just like it," she said, "in the Sypher house in Butte. I noticed it when I was there, in Virgil's old room."

She and Ollie went out, ahead of him.

Cole paid, in a sort of daze. It was not the idea of a poached and cloven bear alone that he reached, as he simultaneously reached the door. The ten curled claws raked his brain. Curled in their hooked sheaths, they looked like nailed, crooked fingers. He felt a ten-fold needle in his eye, the rasp of claws across the whole surface of his mind.